Hero's Call

By
Becca Patterson

Hero's Call

First print edition April, 2015

Acknowledgements

This book was made possible by many people who offered their services and advice. Specifically, I want to thank E. P. Beaumont and Devin Harnois for their insights into the story; my friends Mark and Kamala Wyler for their questions; and especially my husband Ken Justiniano for his understanding and support.

CHAPTER ONE
Kralt

Kayla dodged left then right then left again around people who had no idea how important today was going to be. They wandered along the raised sidewalks out of the way of the motorcars that hurried closer to the speeds Kayla would like to go. Motorcars scared her. How could anyone trust a machine that was so much heavier, faster, and stronger than a person? She preferred to let her own feet hit the pavement than trust her life to one of those beasts. Her opinion was not shared by the people who shared the sidewalks.

In the market square, she had to stop to look for Jarron. He'd said to meet him here today, but the square took up enough space that her people would have called it a village. The square was lined with permanent shops secured to the bases of the trees that lined the opening. All through the middle, in neat, controlled lines with just enough space between for the crowds to pass each other without starting a feud, were tents full of things to buy.

Kayla was tempted to use a portal to put her next to her friend, but she'd already pulled enough attention from the Magisters for her unauthorized use of magic. She didn't dare confront them today. If things went right, she could flip her ears at them on her way out of town and never worry about their silly laws again.

She found Jarron looking at a table filled with clay jars. Seeing him made her heart flutter out of her chest and her stomach clench at the same time. Most people around him let their eyes slide right past him, seeing only the castoff clothes he wore. Kayla focused on his nearly perfect ears that poked up through his waves of hair, twitching ever so slightly as he listened for the hints of threats all around him. He, like her, was a survivor who really didn't have a place in the city.

Last night, she'd managed to hear the thoughts of her sister. Her family waited for her to find a mate and return to take her place among the aunts. She'd sent her own thoughts of Jarron and felt the excitement returned. It destroyed her lingering doubts. She woke sure that today would be her last among the semi-natural structures of the city. Maybe his last, if he said yes.

"Hey," she said before getting too close. She'd seen what he could do when startled.

"Hey." He smiled at her. "What do you think of this one? Perfect for the shelf over the sink, don't you think?" His smile didn't touch his eyes in the least.

He didn't have a shelf, let alone a sink to have a shelf over. He was tracking someone in the crowd. She could see it now in the way his ears twitched.

Kayla couldn't see whom he worried about, but her stomach tightened around the danger. Best then not to say anything that could be considered grounds for questioning by the Magisters.

"It's lovely but won't match the one you bought last week." She slipped her arm around his elbow and pulled him away from the table.

She admired the way their skin contrasted nicely. Hers a pale green from lack of sun. His darker, as though he didn't need the sun. She liked the feel of his skin against hers too. It felt so right, so why was her stomach still tight?

"How are you?" He navigated through the crowd without thinking about it. Walking with Jarron in a crowd could feel as free as walking beside her sister in the steppe.

"I'm happy today." She smiled for him.

"Oh?" He returned the gesture. "Did something happen?"

She pushed aside the thought that he would reject her. "I made a decision. One that will affect you."

His turn to pause while they moved to the edge of the market square. "Is it a good thing?"

"I think so."

He took the time to look about, dropping his pretense of not noticing anything. There were no obvious Magisters about, but anyone could be a snitch.

"Will it get us in trouble?"

She made her own sweep of the people close enough to listen. "Only if we come back."

He nodded. His smile wavered for a moment. Then he pulled her along the path between two shops. "Then ask."

She took a deep breath, her hand going involuntarily to the cramp in her stomach. She couldn't let that stop her now, no matter how nervous she might be.

She stopped so she could look him directly in the eyes. "Will you be my mate and return with me to the steppe?"

His smile lit the alley. "Of course." He pulled her into a hug so tight she wasn't sure her legs were still attached until he set her down. "Wait, you mean your family, as in the Felani?"

She nodded, struggling to stand against the cramp that had seized her stomach. She'd told him weeks ago that she had been abandoned on the edge of the steppe by her mother and taken in by a powerful mage of the tribe. Felani were as different from Kayla as you could get, yet they never once suggest she wasn't part of the tribe, unlike her native people who refused to see Jarron just because he didn't have a home. It had been a struggle learning to walk on only two feet while her sister ran on four. She only had an imaginary tail to control the power the Magisters said she needed a permit to use. Her claws were traded for and lived in tattoos on her arms rather than sheathed in her paws.

"What about my children?" His smile was gone at the thought of the street children he'd pulled together into a tribe of his own. Without him, many of them would be lost to the predators of the city.

"They can"—she had to suck in a breath—"come too."

"Isn't it dangerous?"

She pulled herself up, hands on her hips, trying to stretch her middle. "Only if you don't know how to survive."

"Really?" He all but bounced around like a kit. "We'll be a real family? What do we need? It's not like we have a lot to pack. I'll have to gather them all as soon as possible. They're scattered all over the city by now. Do you mind waiting for night? The kids are easier to find…"

She wanted to answer his questions, but the pain in her stomach radiated out now. This wasn't just nerves seizing around bad food.

"Kayla?"

She couldn't hold enough breath to answer him.

"What's wrong?"

The fear in his eyes scared her. She reached out but pulled back when she saw her arm. Rather, when she saw *through* her arm.

"Jarron?" she cried.

"What's happening?" He grabbed for her, but she didn't feel him against her skin.

There was a tug pulling her chest toward her spine. She reached for him, but her hand passed right through his arm.

Don't panic, she told herself. *You've faced a herd of runners head-on.* That had been, until this moment, the scariest thing she had ever faced.

The tug came again, stronger.

She pulled at the power. Magisters can fly for their rules. The power came, but she couldn't hold it. It danced around her, trying to slide through her bones and blood as it always did. She opened herself to it and felt the tug even harder.

The whole world began to fade, Jarron included. He stood there, tears flowing down his cheeks. His mouth moved with words that didn't reach her ears.

"No, Jarron." She tried again to hold on to him. "I won't leave you." Her hands slid through the space where he had been, but there was nothing there at all.

CHAPTER TWO
Lord Corawin Tromadin

Lord Corawin Tromadin stood in the dusty room under the temple, trying not to breathe too deeply. Priests always used too many herbs and scented oils for their normal rituals, calling on the gods to do the things gods should do because that was their responsibility. He shouldn't have been surprised by the bushels of dried herbs they'd crushed onto the floor and stone slab. They'd dumped almost as many into the fire, then burned more while chanting words that made no sense so they could scatter the ashes over the slab as well.

Lord Callay stood next to him with a cloth held over his nose. "Are you sure about this?" he whispered

"It's too late to back out now."

They had agreed to this plan. He wouldn't let Callay forget that. Callay had to believe he had come up with the idea. Corawin just supplied the details and a set of priests who knew how to call a hero.

"Shouldn't we leave this to the priests?" Callay stifled a sneeze.

"And let the hero think they are in charge?"

Callay didn't look convinced. Corawin wasn't. The ritual was taking far longer than he had planned. The schedule he'd made assumed the hero would be here and have his orders by now. Corawin planned to ride inspection of the peasants this afternoon.

The priests' chants became louder and they formed most of a circle.

"Sire, you must complete the circle." The head priest held out a hand to the lord. The minor priest on the other side was offering his hand to Callay.

5

Corawin steeled himself and took the priest's hand, stepping forward just far enough to complete the circle. When he felt Callay's hand on the other side, something pulled deep in his chest.

"What is that?"

"The hero is fighting us."

"Why would he do that?"

"Because he doesn't know who we are." The priest spoke in the gentle tones one uses with an ignorant child.

Corawin set his jaw and glared at the man. In any other situation, he would have dressed him down immediately for such a transgression. Today, he had to remind himself the ritual had to take precedence even over propriety.

"Then explain it to him." Corawin separated his words carefully, as when dealing with a particularly dense peasant.

The priest took three breaths before responding that any conversation with the hero would be impossible before it took hold. They were just going to have to fight back and let the power and gods do their part.

Corawin only allowed temples and priests in Tromadin County because they were useful for controlling the peasants. That and the law said all magically capable children were to be raised by a temple. Magic had its place, when properly controlled. The problem was with the gods. Gods were too fickle to be considered allies. They did as they pleased whether you prayed to them or not. Their priests were almost as fickle, believing as they did that the god they tended was the wisest of the lot. This led to the idea that they were somehow separate from the hierarchy of lords.

He was beginning to regret his decision to enlist the aid of the priests in finding a hero. There were other ways to find someone capable for his purposes that didn't involve the feeling of power he couldn't control surging through his chest.

The shadow of a body appeared on the stone table, and the intensity of the anger surging through him grew stronger. He could feel a heart beating separate from his own, hard but slow. With each beat of that heart, the shadow became more solid. Shifting from shadow to translucent ghost and finally into a solid body breathing evenly as though asleep. Three breaths before the power left his chest with only his own heart slamming against his ribs.

That was no hero.

It wore no armor. The chest that rose and fell with breath, while not well endowed, wasn't flat either. Pointed ears poked out through the blue tinged hair that was allowed to flow freely from its head. What little clothing it did wear would have scandalized a common whore. It was a flimsy flowery frock that barely reached its knees and didn't even try to cover its arms.

"It's green." He turned toward the head priest, fighting to keep his hands from strangling the man.

"It's the hero you specified." He faced Corawin with bravery few men could muster.

"Ha." Callay had the scented cloth back up to his nose. "That is a demon, not a hero."

The priest shifted to look at both lords at once, putting his back to the green demon they had just pulled from the abyss.

"You did not specify that you wanted a human man." There was no fear in his voice. His eyes told a different story, shifting rapidly between the lords. "Heroes come in many shapes and sizes. Had the skills you asked for been those of a dragon, a dragon would have appeared on that slab."

The demon twitched; everyone took a step back.

"Principe, I asked for someone capable of infiltrating the palace. That will stick out like a sore thumb. What am I to do with it?"

The priest watched the demon now. "Hire her. Only when she fulfills her mission will the spell end and send her back where she came from."

Any answer Corawin might have offered died in his throat when the demon flipped itself into a crouched stance with six knifes held between her fingers. It was clear now that her arms and legs were out of proportion to her body. There was no way someone with such awkward limbs could be the kind of skilled fighter he needed.

"Hara grin taka sroat." Her eyes, slit like a cat's, bored into Corawin.

She knows power when she sees it, Corawin thought. *Maybe I can turn this to my advantage.*

"I am Lord Corawin Tromadin, Lord of Tromadin County." He paused to let her bow, which she didn't. "I've summoned you to protect our kingdom from our king. He and his family have become corrupt and must be removed from power for the good of the country."

The demon watched him through his entire speech without so much as a twitch.

"I don't think she appreciates your offer." Lord Callay lowered his cloth just long enough to catch the demon's attention. He put the cloth back in place and backed into the wall when her eyes pierced him.

"We are willing to pay you for your time and talent." Corawin pulled her attention back. Callay may have given the coin for this operation, but Corawin wasn't about to let him take any of the credit.

The sounds that came from her throat were unlike any language he'd heard, even from the barbarians who traveled about in garish carts, selling exotic holdrums to anyone with more coin than sense.

"Principe." Corawin snarled at the head priest. "You talk sense into her."

The priest nodded and stepped forward. With more gestures than were seemly, he uttered greetings in several different languages. She responded to none of them. Another of the priests came forward and offered words in more languages than Corawin could imagine. Why the world needed so many ways to say anything was beyond him. The rest of the countries should quit trying to be unique and learn the common tongue of Greylein. It would make so many things easier.

"Farrit!" She jumped down from the table, landing lightly on her feet in front of Corawin. "Farrit de jama!" She snarled in his face.

She came close enough that Corawin was forced to smell her breath and skin. The scent was stomach turning. She smelled vaguely of copper and roses with a hint of something carnivorous. Her hand came up with one finger extended. She'd managed to sheathe her knives unnoticed. In the space of a heartbeat that lasted too long, she poked his nose and jumped back.

"Hessen grit moriat." She spoke this time to Callay, then turned to Principe Haverey. "Musse ly moriat."

She stood up straight. In this position, it was easy to miss the ungainliness of her arms and legs. She pulled herself slowly to her full height. Her dress, no more than a flimsy night frock at best, barely reached her knees. Her eyes passed around the room and landed back on Corawin with an intensity that was sure to visit his dreams. Then she turned and walked toward the door.

"Wait!" Corawin reached for her, but she slapped his hand aside.

Her other hand came up under his chin, three points pressed against the skin there.

"Guards," Callay screamed. "Guards."

Corawin's personal guards rushed through the door, fanning into a defensive wedge. They had trained this maneuver to block the door and give them the best vantage to assess a situation. The lead guard's eyes lit on the hero just in time for him to fall through a blue hole in the floor and reappear through a similar mark in the ceiling. The rest of his guards advanced around the hole toward the demon.

She moved fast, disemboweling the first before he could strike, then slipping through another blue hole. The second guard thrust his sword after her and lost half the blade when the hole disappeared. She was now on the other side of the room, using the stone table as a shield. The guards fought past the priests who were fleeing the demon they had called. The room was filled with blue holes that appeared wherever it would be advantageous to the demon.

She worked her way back across the room, slashing at anyone who made it past her little blue holes.

"Stop her."

The guards who were still standing had grown wary of her blades and the holes. She made it out the door just before one of those holes filled the entire frame.

"After her."

The guards hesitated. One stepped through when Corawin drew his own sword. That guard stumbled through a similar hole that now graced the far wall.

"By all that's holy…" Principe Haverey clasped his Eye of Odran and held it to his forehead.

"It's just magic." Corawin scoffed at the priest. "Can't you do something about it?"

Haverey stepped back. "I can't see or feel this power."

"What difference does that make? She's your creation. Do something." Corawin pushed the priest back.

Just then the pair of holes through which one of his guards was continually falling closed, splitting the man in half and scattering him over the room. Callay wretched. The priests mumbled their prayers with their medallions pressed to their foreheads. The guards lost their postures and just stared at the door.

"We're trapped," someone whispered.

Corawin fought the urge to agree.

"You and you." He pointed to the least injured of the guards. "Get the grate out of that window." He ordered one of the priests to tend to the wounded and the rest to begin cleaning up the mess. "Principe, I hope you can track her."

"What are you going to do?" Callay looked almost as green as the demon but held himself with dignity.

"Convince her to help us." Corawin hated the idea of hiring a woman for a man's job, but why hire a man for a demon's job? She'd just shown him what a demon could do.

"You still think this is a good idea?"

Corawin smiled. "Yes, it's an even better idea now."

CHAPTER THREE
Kayla

Kayla ran through the firelit stone tunnels. Her heart pounded in her chest, from fear more than effort. The charm didn't work. The words that would send a demon back to their icy realms had no effect. They hadn't even flinched.

Neala had scared her as a kit with tales of the demons who walked like Techan, but with short stubby legs and arms that couldn't quite reach all the way around. They were demons born in the ice, with skin the color of grass gone dry, who waited for someone to misbehave and create a hole between the worlds. She'd believed in them until she was old enough to hunt on her own. They were just a children's story to keep the kits from running wild in the night.

Except they were real.

They stood over her, wrapped in robes that made a mockery of the Magisters. They growled at her, their arms waving about in weird ways. When she tried to leave, they revealed their real purpose. Just as Neala had said, they were going to sacrifice her to open the gate for more of their kind.

It took most of her reserves to get out of that room, and just barely at that. Her trick with the portals wouldn't last long, and they would hunt her down. She had to get beyond their reach and truly break their connection.

These stone tunnels ran forever, just not in any one direction. They met at angles, with nothing to tell one tunnel from the rest. There were no markers that she could see that would lead her out of this hell. There were no anchors to anything familiar. She had just enough power left for one, maybe two portals if she didn't reconnect with the source.

Run.

Run as far and as fast as she could, even within these tunnels. To stop would be to die.

The thought tempted her for one heartbeat while she faced yet another cross tunnel. Her next thought was of Jarron vibrating with excitement when she asked him to go home with her. She had to live. She would make it back to him and the children.

Their faces filled her mind as she continued to run. Each one a precious kit abandoned as she had been. She was lucky to have a family with aunts to tell her stories and teach her to hunt for the tribe. She had uncles who cleaned her scrapes and taught her how not to fall. They were lucky to find each other. And Jarron.

The city didn't make a space for the abandoned children. It swept them aside and pretended they didn't exist. Just the same as the Magisters ignoring her abilities and telling her she needed to be properly trained in the use of power. She had clashed with the Magisters and their rules from the start. Most bowed to their power and accepted their fate.

Kayla would not.

She wouldn't accept the restrictions of the Magisters, nor would she accept the role the demons chose for her.

She had learned long ago that not having a tail didn't mean she couldn't wield power. All it meant was she had to be creative. The same when it came to hunting. She couldn't run like her sisters to keep up with the beasts of the planes. Some had laughed at the idea that she would even try. They didn't laugh when she brought home *two* great elk on her solo hunt.

This was just the same. She had to be creative. She had to do what she could to get the results she wanted. Like twisting the power around an imaginary tail or using portals to confuse the great elk so she could walk up and slit their throats.

These tunnels were made by demons. They were spelled to be confusing. So she had to find a way to ignore the tunnels and find her way out. She slowed as she approached the next turn, closed her eyes, and listened.

Clanging from the demons in their metal armor rang through the tunnels. Time was not her friend. She stood still in the cross path, eyes closed, and let her other senses feel the space. The demons were too loud, so she ignored her ears as well. A light breeze tickled her eyelashes from the right.

No time for thought, she ran in that direction and found a set of stairs leading up toward a light that didn't come from the smoky torches that lined the tunnels.

Kayla stumbled up the stairs set too low for comfort and too wide to take two at a time. She had to slow herself to keep from tripping. Landing flat out or injuring herself would give the demons what they wanted. One step at a time, as quickly as she could move her feet. The light came from around a poorly sealed door.

She burst out into the light of day. The sun burned brighter than she expected. It took some time to get used to the direct light. Much like the height of summer at noon in the steppe, but she hadn't been there in years. In Kralt, the sun was always filtered by the leaves overhead. She'd grown too used to that.

All around her, she heard screams and voices like the ones in the chamber below. The people here were in danger, and she couldn't see to join the fight. Slowly her eyes cleared. She moved away from the door into the streets. Shapes became people, running in all directions. People cleared into demons. The demons screamed as they dove out of her way.

How many demons were there?

CHAPTER FOUR
Allay

Allay opened her eyes in the dark of her little closet next to the kitchen. The sound of Cook loading wood into the oven told her it was time to be awake and in the real world. This morning she was happy to leave the dream world behind. It was fun to be a hunter, tracking down great beasts for her tribe to feast on. But the beasts were all tinged green and unlike anything she'd seen before. They hid in the grasses that were purple and as tall as she was.

In the dream, Allay had a family waiting at home for her to make her first solo kills. She could feel them watching from the sheltered hollow where they had set camp for the season. She set her sights on a pair of great beasts, young males not quite old enough to leave the herd, but old enough to linger on the edges. She imagined a small group of her sisters as great cats, prowling through the grass, and they became almost real. Real enough to startle the herd and chase them right toward the place she was hiding in the grass. She let most of the herd pass, jumping out just in time to slash the throat of the young male as he ran past with the knives that came to her hand like claws when she closed her fist. The other veered away from her, running at a cross angle to the rest of the herd.

Allay only smiled and thought of a portal that appeared in front of the beast and brought him back to where she was ready to slash his throat too. The sun hadn't yet made it halfway to the top of the sky. She could continue her hunt and bring home more than the family could eat, but that would be wasteful. Going home so early would be boastful.

She woke to the sounds of Cook preparing the kitchen before she could decide what to do. *Just as well,* Allay thought. She rose and dressed as quickly as she could in the little space before Cook could come in and tell her to get up. She folded blankets and rolled them into her mattress, which fit neatly under the lowest shelf. Sure that all signs of her life in the little closet were hidden away, she slipped into the kitchen.

"Good morning, child." Cook flashed her a bright smile. "Breakfast will be ready when you get back."

Allay bobbed a quick curtsy to acknowledge Cook's message. She didn't have to look to know why Cook was in a good mood. There was only one traveler in the inn last night, and he'd asked for the quiet room at the end of the hall. Cook would be embarrassed if she knew Allay knew what they did on the quiet nights.

There was a chill in the air this morning. Not enough to freeze the top of the cistern, but there was frost on the tips of the grass that grew around the edges of the yard. It was getting harder to ignore that winter was coming. At least the stifling heat of summer was past for the most part. Frost meant the worst of the insects would die off, and more travelers would choose to sleep in a warm inn rather than in their wagons in the market square.

Allay checked the level in the cistern (half full) and the wood-pile (waist high) on her way back for breakfast. She would need to head out for more wood if she could get it today. Allay filled the pail from the cistern halfway up and chose the small stick to bring to Cook. Allay couldn't speak, but that didn't mean she never had anything to say.

You'll be better off getting wood today, Cook thought when she saw the message in Allay's hands.

Allay held up the pail, then handed the stick to Cook.

"You are a smart child, no matter what anyone says." Cook filled a bowl with porridge and sent Allay to the little table in the nook by the oven. She'd already set out the honey and dried fruits. "One quick trip to the city well early will be a good idea, then out to the woods with you."

Cook didn't know Allay could hear her thoughts, and Allay had no way to tell her. Their language of gestures and signs only went so far. Not that Allay would dare complain. She was loved, which was more than she could say for some of the children in the city streets. Praise was rare enough for all the motherless children. She took it with a smile.

"Good morning, my loves." Missy came in with a kiss for Cook and a hug for Allay. "How many towels are in there today?" Missy

16

asked when she squeezed Allay's bodice.

Allay held up five fingers while pursing her lips.

"Five still?" Missy gave her a sad smile. "Never fear, you will grow into it. You just have to wait for your time." *It's better than wearing a child's frock.*

Allay got the impression Missy knew. There were days when the customers were being particularly cruel in their minds about the "poor mute girl" and how horrible it was for the women of the inn to be doubly burdened with a child not theirs and a cripple on top of that. Missy gave her more love on those days.

"Water and wood today?" Missy asked, seeing the bucket and stick on the shelf by the door. "I suppose that would be best. Keep you out of the way while we clean." Missy ladled her own bowl of porridge and joined Cook and Allay at the table.

"Are you expecting a crowd?" Cook asked.

"I've heard rumors." Missy poured honey over her porridge and thought about men in armor.

Allay tried not to see too much in Missy's mind, but some thoughts were just too loud to ignore.

"I'll be wanting extra bread, then?" Cook imagined the same kind of men.

How they did that Allay never could tell. They didn't read each other's minds, not the way Allay did. If they did, they would have known what she could and couldn't hear. No, Missy hadn't meant to share what some men would do to a girl they thought couldn't report them or even scream while they did it. Still, it was nice sometimes to know what they were thinking.

If there were soldiers coming to the capital, they would need a full stock of wood and water. Allay slurped her porridge as quick as she could. The sooner she got to the well, the sooner she could get out of the city.

"Keep yourself safe today," Missy called out the kitchen door while Allay dragged the water wagon from its place beside the shed.

Allay nodded and smiled. She waved when she had the cart ready to go. Missy waved from the kitchen door. Cook would already be up to her elbows in bread dough.

The cart bounced along the street as she ran to the well. The only other traffic here this early in the morning was the other shop children heading out on their errands. Allay waved to the ones who were friendly. Her friends, like her, had been adopted by the shop owners to help with the running of the shops. Children were cheaper than hired hands. Most of them were well cared for. Most, not all. Yet it was still better to be a shop child with a full load of duties than a street child who never knew when they would eat next.

Allay wished she could tell someone about the bruises no one else saw.

The children at the well knew the rules. You helped the people ahead of you draw their water and the ones who came later would help you draw yours. This early in the morning there were no adults who didn't understand the way things worked. Allay took her place on the rope to pull the bucket up. Each cart was filled as full as the child driving it could handle. Four carts ahead of her, then hers was filled likewise.

The children talked and thought about the rumors Missy had mentioned. Some of the shops were preparing for extra customers. Some were planning to close. A few thought the rumors nonsense. It was the day after Holy Obligation. Who would bring soldiers to the capital today?

Allay never understood what the soldiers or nobles who ordered them around thought. Soldiers who came to the inn didn't want to think about their orders—they were on a break. The nobles were never close enough for her to hear their thoughts at all.

The barrel cart didn't bounce on the way back to the Broken Ale. It trundled along, looking for any hole to fall into. Allay managed to get it back to the yard without losing too much water. Cook had her hands full of bread while Missy dished out the porridge to the quiet morning crowd. Allay emptied the water and grabbed her harness for the wood.

"Don't forget your lunch." Cook nodded to a small sack on the corner of the baking table.

Allay went around the table to hug Cook before grabbing the sack. It was small enough that no one would think she was carrying anything too valuable but large enough to hold more than one meal's worth of Cook's bread and cheese with a few of the cookies Cook made specially for the griffins. No one would mistake them for a treat; they were disgusting for anyone who wasn't a griffin.

"Keep yourself safe out there." Missy stood in the door between the kitchen and the common room. Her arms were folded across her chest, the way she did when she had something to worry about. The only thought Allay saw was an image of herself asleep in a pile of fur and feathers.

Those rumors she wasn't thinking about must be something if she meant for Allay to stay out overnight.

"And take your cloak," Cook said before Allay could leave.

"You never know about the weather this time of year." Cook imagined Allay in a cave with the cloak for a blanket and a little fire not far off to keep her warm.

Allay grabbed her cloak and smiled to them both, then left before they could remind her of anything else. The streets were full now. Even the people who didn't have work were out and about. Their thoughts bumped into each other until Allay couldn't hear any one thought. There were advantages to being in a crowd, though the din gave her a headache after a while.

"A little late for wood gathering?" The guard at the gate looked at her with disapproval.

Allay focused on his eyes for just a moment to find that he too was concerned about something that would be coming close to the end of the day.

"Just make sure you're back in time for the gate closing." He gave her a sympathetic smile. *Poor child, asked to do more than she should.*

Allay turned away before he could see the look on her face. He was just like all the rest. She couldn't speak. She was still perfectly capable of everything else a girl her age should be. More so, since she could hear the thoughts of adults to help her understand what they wanted her to do. One thing she understood was it did no good to show your anger to a guard.

She couldn't tell him she was off to play with the griffins. They were always up for a game, and if Missy and Cook had expected her back before gate closing, she could return with a full load of wood before the end of his shift. She couldn't tell him that. He wouldn't understand that griffins aren't just silly creatures who like to nest near human cities.

Allay walked away from the gate, keeping to the road until she was sure the guard wasn't watching her anymore. Then she skipped off the road into the tangled grasses around the city. *I've come to play,* she thought to her winged friends.

CHAPTER FIVE
Lord Corawin Tromadin

Getting clear of the mess the demon had left had been annoying. More annoying was the way she had left trails going every which way in the dust of the passages below the temple. The men had split up to follow every lead. If he'd been smart, he would have just made everyone stand still and listen. They would have heard the women screaming and known it had escaped the tunnels.

Summoned demons weren't supposed to be able to leave hallowed ground without permission. Another reason not to trust the temples, or rather the priests. The fact that a priest could have been born to any manner of family, or even no family at all, was enough to distrust them. But they claimed any child who had the potential for magic, which gave them power that couldn't be ignored or substituted.

"My lord." The pompous man who called himself the village mayor all but ran up to him as soon as he stepped into the sunlight.

Demons weren't supposed to be able to survive in direct sunlight. That, it seemed, was another fallacy.

"I'm indisposed at the moment." Corawin waved off the man.

"There was a green beast that came from that very door just two minutes ago." The man never had been good at taking a hint, even when it was clubbed into his head.

"That's why I'm indisposed." Corawin waved one of the guards forward to deal with the fat fool.

If the mayor had enough to grow fat on, this village's taxes weren't high enough. He'd have to look into that. Later.

"Where did she go?" The priest stepped around Corawin to

speak directly to the peasant.

The man and most of the crowd that gathered around all pointed east. East toward Lake Thorn and Greylein City. It was too much to hope that the demon would do as he wanted without being instructed. He swallowed the temptation to kill the principe here. It would just cause more trouble than it was worth.

"Bring my horse and catch up."

He set out on foot, looking for tracks he could identify as hers. There hadn't been a single clear print in the dust below the temple. And here in the street, there were too many people trampling over anything.

The panicking people and animals sufficed until he walked past the edge of town. The road became nothing more than a pair of trenches in the grass. His passage left nothing discernible in that kind of dirt.

"Sir." A man brought his horse. "The dogs are on their way." He bowed, then stood awkwardly for a moment. "They are trying to get her scent from the stone slab."

Dogs were a good idea. He must have suggested it. They should have been faster about it though. He didn't want to deal with the scandal if word of this made it back to the council. It was bad enough that Callay knew about it. He, at least, was involved enough to be caught in the scandal as well.

He would have to start planting blame on one of his rivals. Farthingay for example. He let a smile sneak across his lips at the thought. Nothing would please him more than to see that man brought low by a demon. He was such a staunch believer in the righteousness of his position. He had to be hiding some dirty secrets. The right rumors planted before an accusation could be devastating to one as annoyingly innocent as that man.

The dogs came howling on the trail of the demon. Corawin vaulted into his saddle in time to take a comfortable seat before the dogs ran past his horse. Even a well-trained horse would shy at that kind of chaos. The trick was learning to move with the horse. He reasserted control as soon as the dogs were past, then followed after them. The handlers were still behind him when the pack stopped their wild run. Their howls diminished to whimpers as they sniffed around the ground.

"What now?" Corawin pierced the nearest handler with a look that made the man quiver.

"They've lost the trail, sir."

"How could they lose the trail?"

"We'll know when they find it again." He bowed and scurried

away to tend to his dogs.

Blast it all. They were in the middle of an open meadow. Recently grazed by the look of it. The tallest of the grasses barely reached his toes as he walked his horse around the site. What could possibly have covered the trail out here? It wasn't like it could have shimmied up a tree and left her scent out of reach of the dogs. The nearest trees were at the horizon, where Lake Thorn sat as the boundary between his lands and the royal county that surrounded the capital.

That tree line was nearly a day's ride away, despite the appearance. If it weren't for the edicts declaring Lake Thorn off-limits to all commercial activity save special fishing expeditions, there would have been a town of inns on the shore. Corawin usually took the southern road to the capital rather than camp rough by the lake. Would the demon have seen the lake as something tempting or revolting? The stories would offer no guidance; they'd been wrong about everything except its color so far.

A dog's bark interrupted his thoughts. A handler was there in a moment.

"Sir."

Corawin dropped to the ground as he approached the spot. He knew he wasn't going to like it before he saw it.

The dog sat beside a circle of dirt where the grasses and whatever else had been there were gone. Maybe she'd taken herself off to home, though that wasn't likely.

"Spread out and find her."

"Sir?" The men gathered around, none willing to touch that circle of dirt—even the dog handlers who hadn't been in the temple to see the blue disks the demon made.

"What are you waiting for?"

"What do we do when we find her?"

"Catch her and bring her to me." *Idiots.* "If that's not possible, *kill* her and bring her to me." Corawin let his tone tell them how upset he was. The men never seemed to work any harder than his level of frustration.

The soldiers divided themselves into hunting parties and moved off in search of a demon who could pass through walls and drop herself through blue disks. They would need the help of all the gods to complete this task, and heavens if the gods weren't paying attention. He left them to their impossible task while he took on his.

He burst through the main temple doors, yelling for Principe Haverey. Other priests were in the middle of their afternoon prayers. They glared at him for the interruption. He glared back for their rudeness.

"My lord?" Haverey appeared before Corawin could draw enough breath to holler again.

"Prepare the temple to house the entire village."

"What for?" Haverey drew himself up to his full height and then some before remembering to say, "Sir?"

Corawin held back the slap that man so richly deserved. There would be time enough to deal with his insubordination after the demon was under control. How he'd been made principe with such a dull wit was just another on the list of reasons to hate this man.

"The demon will return. I don't need another panic while we dispose of her."

"Sire, that is more than we contracted for."

"I still haven't received the hero I commissioned. Until that happens, the contract is unresolved."

"You got what you asked for." The principe stepped back slightly. "No one ever promised it would come exactly as you expected."

Corawin stepped into the priest's personal space until the man was backed up against a pillar. "I asked for a hero, not a monster who would menace my people."

"She has the ability to do as you ask."

"But not the ability to understand." Corawin grabbed the priest's robes and twisted them tight around his neck. "Prepare your temple."

Corawin dropped him as suddenly as he'd grabbed him. The way the priest leaned against the pillar to save himself from falling to the ground amused Corawin, but not enough to make him smile.

CHAPTER SIX
Kayla

Kayla shivered in the shade of the trees on the little island she'd found after dropping herself in the lake. Her shoes were at the bottom of the lake where she'd dropped them to lose their weight. Not that she needed shoes except in the cold of winter. She'd learned to hunt by feeling the beat of hooves on the ground. That wouldn't help her here on the island, but the water would prevent most forms of tracking from following her.

Uncle Threshin, leader of the hunt classes, had made all the kits practice being prey before they ever learned a single skill for hunting.

"You need to be able to think like an elk or a rabbit in order to catch one."

All the kits of her class laughed at that, until he sent them out into the steppe with the tribe's best hunters on their trail. If you could make it until sundown without getting caught, you would pass into the hunting phase of the training.

Kayla was the first kit of her tribe, in all of the stories leading back beyond living memory, to ever pass that test on her first try.

The other kits complained of cheating. The hunters were equally frustrated. Even after she'd told them how she'd spent more years than any of them watching the hunts and learning, they still insisted on a special test for her. This time the elders watched by scrying as she confused her scent and moved in unexpected ways. When she returned at moonrise still untagged by the hunters, Father declared Kayla had the makings of an expert hunter.

She'd never once thought she'd need to use these skills for

anything more than a mental exercise to understand her prey. Yet here she was, hiding her scent trail and refusing to start a fire to keep herself hidden. She could shiver herself warm enough to make the danger of being caught more than the danger of being cold. Once the sun dried her dress, she'd be able to use that as well, for what little it would provide.

The dress was ruined. Caked in mud with splatters of red blood from the demons she'd cut. She'd been surprised to notice they had failed to cut her, for all their trying. Or perhaps this water had healing properties. She didn't believe that, but the first chance she'd had to check herself for injuries came after she dropped into the lake. She had no cuts or scrapes from their weapons. There were a couple rips in the delicate fabric of the dress, but that could have come from the grass she ran through.

Jarron bought her that dress. Well, he said he bought it, but if he'd paid for it, it had been with money he'd stolen. That would have bothered her if the people of Kralt had even pretended to care about the labor that made their things. Most of them didn't even know what it took work to make cloth, or cut it in the right shapes, or sew it together properly. They believed in machines. Machines didn't need to have their work respected—according to the people.

Of course, the people also didn't think people like Jarron needed to be respected. With no respect going in any direction, she didn't really care how he had acquired the dress. He respected her enough to give it to her so she could pass in the city as one of the people and get the kind of respect they would never give to him.

"I just want you to have the best chance to complete your quest," he told her when he gave it to her. "I just want to help."

He helped. He showed her exactly what she was looking for, without trying to be what she wanted. She still didn't known whom she was looking for when he became her perfect match.

The sun sank under the horizon while she imagined Jarron sitting beside her. Even here, in this hell, she could be happy with him by her side. That he wasn't by her side made this worse than hell.

"Don't think I'll just give up." She hoped the spirits could hear her. "Have your fun, but I'll get him back in the end."

***

Sleep didn't find her in the dark for a long time. Long enough for her to map out the stars overhead. There were heroes in the stars of this world, but she couldn't find them. None of the stories she knew were evident here, just like the source. There had to be a source here; she just couldn't find it.

It wouldn't kill her to learn to live without magic. Auntie Harmiline told of a tribe beyond the jungles in the south who considered use of the source to be yagram—evil. Somehow she'd managed to find her mate there. Uncle Heram refused to learn the ways of the source. There were some who called him crazy but ate his kills as readily as anyone else's. He showed how strong one could become if they didn't rely on the source.

Kayla watched him closely when she thought she would be unable to wield power because she didn't have a tail. Even when she did learn to take that power and bend it to her will, she never forgot the body had its own power, if it were trained properly. Hers was different from her tribe's, so she had to figure out many things on her own. No one could teach her how to balance on two legs or manipulate things with her fingers. They couldn't teach her how to run more efficiently, nor could they match her for endurance.

Morning woke her from uneasy dreams of pink demons infesting the purple grasses of her home. Hunger also made its presence known. At home, this wouldn't have been a problem. Even in the jungles, she knew how to spot edible leaves and catch the small animals that would provide enough meat for one. Here, nothing was the right color and the small animals smelled disgusting.

It was all so confusing. She pulled the last of her power into a net cast over the island to test and report of anything that wouldn't kill her. There were plenty of options, but the most appetizing were the little red berries that ripened unmolested on the bush. They were bitter with a peppery aftertaste that wouldn't wash away with just water. She waited an hour for any ill effects to show up before filling her pockets with more of the little berries. The reddish green leaves of a large tree tasted even worse, but they stained her fingers pink.

She gathered more of those leaves and stuffed them between her breasts. A little dye might help her blend in, so long as it didn't bother her skin too much. Not that she could become exactly like the stumpy-limbed demons, but she might pass unnoticed at a distance.

That gave her an idea. Not all prey ran when confronted by a predator. Some stood so still they couldn't be seen. Some never strayed far from their warrens, trusting the construction of their home to save them from a toothy death. Aside from the lack of food, which might be the same everywhere, Kayla could make this little island her bolt-hole. So long as none saw her here, she'd be safe. For a while.

CHAPTER SEVEN
Allay

Allay woke with a feather tickling her nose. The warmth that covered her was almost stifling if it wasn't for all the love that flowed through the pile of griffins. It must be about time to open the inn and get breakfast started. Today, though, she could slide back into her dreams, weird though they may be.

She dreamed again of the place where the colors were all wrong. This time she ran with the large catlike creatures through the red grasses while the runner beasts scrambled to get out of the way. They weren't hunting this time. This was her family and they were moving to the summer grounds.

The dreams are different. Sharl shifted under her.

I didn't mean to wake you. Allay took the opportunity to shift her position.

Sharl laughed. *Of course not. You never do. But you aren't the only one having strange dreams.*

Griffins all around her began to shift and stretch where they could. Most of them agreed about the strange dreams from this pile. Some thought they should remember this arrangement so they could do it again. Others wanted to remember so they wouldn't dream that way again.

There was still dew on the grass when Allay tumbled from her place deep within the griffin pile. They would never let her anywhere near the edge of a pile—she didn't have enough feathers or fur to protect her or the rest of the pile. *Besides,* Sharl pointed out, *you are a guest. We can't expect you to protect us when your mothers send you to our protection.*

One problem with staying with the griffins was she had to sleep in her clothes. The bodice was comfortable as much as such a thing can be when you're still too small for it. She had to take it off to readjust the towels and get a little air to her chemise. No sense in complaining, though; she could take a good long stretch this morning and no one would see her being so indecent.

Can you make a fire? Have you learned to cook rabbits? Sharl pranced next to her. Her head was filled with the smell of rabbits.

I don't have any seasonings. Allay imagined the dried herbs Cook always used on the rabbits they got in at the inn when there were fancy people about.

Make your fire, careful. Sharl thought of the spot to the woodward side of the great rock where Allay hid the harness she'd made for flying. Sharl took off to catch up with the rest of the griffins soaring high into the sky and turning lazy circles that became wild patterns between them. It was impossible to follow her in the swirls of wings.

The fire crackled merrily behind the great rock when Sharl returned with a pair of rabbits in her beak and a new story in her mind. Allay took the rabbits and let Sharl show her new story.

A green woman with pointed ears ran through a town, scaring people who stumbled over themselves to get out of the way. The woman seemed just as scared as the people who were screaming, but she was much more skilled than they were in avoiding collisions. She dodged the big farmers who tried to stop her and slid under the horses whose riders had abandoned them. She made it out of the town without killing anyone—human or otherwise—and then came the big moment. The woman stopped, looked around, then fell through a blue hole that vanished as soon as she was gone.

What monster is that? Allay asked as she set the rabbit on a stick over the little flames.

She's not a monster. Sharl pulled herself up proud with chest feathers puffed out. *She's a hero. The lord chasing her said so.*

Allay looked up at her friend in disbelief. She searched her mind, as much as she would let her, for evidence of teasing. She should know better by now. Griffins don't lie, even to tease each other. It's too easy to catch a lie when you share thoughts.

Where did she come from?

Sharl's feathers drooped. Her version of a shrug. The story had been passed around the griffins as they hunted for breakfast. Allay couldn't trace the source of the story, but it was clear the images weren't just imagined.

Where did she go?

The lord would like to know that too. She shook her head. *Are you going to eat?*

Allay laughed. The rabbit wasn't quite done yet. *What games are you planning?*

It feels like a lake day. The air was warming quickly with a clear sky. And the thought of fresh fish for lunch made Allay laugh again.

Allay survived the game of tag that erupted on the way to Lake Thorn. She thanked several gods for the wisdom to insist on more than griffin magic to keep her in place as they soared, dove, and whirled through the sky. She added a plea to those same gods to remind her to bring her winter leathers any time she was out with the griffins. Never mind the few who insisted on teasing her about having to wear any sort of fabric at all. They didn't mean anything by it other than to preen their own egos and feathers.

Given the chance, Allay would have taken feathers over clothes. Though she wouldn't give up her arms and fingers for wings. She liked being able to sew and cut her food into bite-sized bits. Sharl was always willing to take her up whenever she had time.

Wait. Allay tugged at Sharl's feathers when she realized they'd switched to fishing.

What? She took a moment to realize she wouldn't survive the way the griffins dove into the water. *Where do you want me to set you?*

Allay looked over the lake. Islands dotted the center, one of them big enough to suggest berry patches that wouldn't be molested by bears or deer. It also had enough trees to give her shelter. Maybe even a small fire so she would be ready to roast a fish for herself.

Sharl left her on the beach of the island and joined the others who were churning the water. Allay watched them, not sure they really *needed* to fly so high before diving into the lake. Considering how many times they resurfaced without a fish, she wasn't sure this kind of fishing was any good at all. They were having fun. It was fun just to watch them drag themselves from the lake, shaking the water off their wings, and rise into the sky before plummeting with a shriek. Unlike the morning hunt for rabbits and other small animals, this was as much about being loud as it was about catching fish.

They are trying to kill me! The thought hit Allay's mind like a blow from behind. There weren't words so much as the feeling of complete dread at the sight of the griffins diving all around the lake.

Allay turned to find the source of the thought. She came face to face with the creature in Sharl's story this morning.

She froze, her eyes caught by the creature's eyes. They looked normal, until you noticed the slit irises. Her legs were longer than they

31

should be, and so were her arms. They looked like they would get in the way, except she held them with such grace it was almost beautiful. Beautiful right down to the tips of the curved knives she held between her fingers.

What are you? Never before had Allay wished she had a voice as much as this moment.

The thoughts that came back were the images from her dreams. Especially the tall, red grasses and catlike creatures.

My dreams, my friends' dreams.

My home.

The woman stood up all the way, her long legs pushing her up taller than Allay expected. Her dress was mud-covered and torn so short her knees showed below what was left of the skirt. The sleeves were also missing, leaving her arms bare and proving the green went all the way.

Allay's mind was filled with stars and images of balls that spun around each other with a sense of curiosity. There were stars in the distance, but they weren't where they were supposed to be. Allay pushed all the balls away and pulled the stars into the pictures she knew.

CHAPTER EIGHT
Kayla

The little demon had a strong mind, even if her thoughts were as strange as this whole world. She tried as best as she could to turn Kayla's questions into answers, but she wasn't practiced in mind speech, nor did she know much about the universe beyond the stars she could see in the night sky.

What the little demon did was show Kayla they weren't all crazy fighters who couldn't wield a sword against a tree. She also showed Kayla there weren't only demons in this world. The crazy creatures made of fur and feathers weren't attacking her, but the fish that populated the lake. And they were also able to understand the touch of a familiar mind.

The griffins' thoughts followed a pattern similar to the ones she was most familiar with. They knew even less about the stars or the magic that brought her here. They thought she was a fun novelty and showed her the story of her run from the temple. For that story, they owed her a fish. They were off competing to see who could bring the fish back first.

Kayla didn't tell them she couldn't eat the fish.

Why not? The little demon had lost all her fear in favor of curiosity.

I am different. Kayla sent more details, but the girl rejected most of them as unintelligible. She tried to fit them into the things she knew, but they just didn't match.

I'm different too. The girl had been born without a voice among people who where mind-mutes. She infused the thought with all the pain of being isolated among her own people.

Are there none to teach you to focus your thoughts?

The girl played that thought around in her mind, not quite rejecting it.

The connections she showed Kayla were of men and women dressed in different kinds of clothes—similar to the way the Magisters set themselves apart from the populations of the cities. Allay, the girl's name came in a memory of one such priest, thought of these people with respect and honor. These priests did their best with Allay as she grew, but all they knew was magic, and Allay had none.

They can't hear me.

Kayla felt her heart open to this child. Always, there were children left to fend for themselves. Not on the steppe, not in the northern reaches where the Krinna kept to their villages. With her own people and now the demons, there were children who should have been loved and raised with all the support they needed.

They love me! Allay stood suddenly, knocking the berries she gathered to the ground. The two women who ran an inn and took Allay as their own filled Kayla's mind until they blocked out every other thought. Kayla learned many details about these women before Allay's power faded.

Of course they love you. Kayla pushed calm toward the child.

They returned to their gathering of berries. Allay took only the dark-blue ones, avoiding the red ones that Kayla liked with the care of one who'd been hurt by something.

These berries, what are they? Kayla rolled one around in her fingers.

Poison. Demons died quickly with even a single berry or if the juice touched a cut. None of these were actual memories from the child; they were borrowed from someone.

A pair of griffins crashed through the trees to land in spaces that should not have been able to hold them. There was a golden-plumed female with a large fish of one species in her beak and a smaller blue-green male with a larger fish of a different species.

They were each claiming to have reached "the hero" first.

Kayla laughed and declared a tie before accepting the fish. She thanked them both for their effort. They took off again, somehow slipping through the branches of the trees. It was more of that magic she couldn't see; it had to be.

You can use magic? Allay looked up at her with the awe of a kit who hadn't yet felt the tug of the source. *What's it like?*

Kayla thought of the feeling of the source. On her world, it was an always-present feeling of warmth and tingles in the back of her mind. It filled her with energy. Here, she felt deflated with the lack of power.

There is power here. Allay thought of all the priests who could make things move without touching them, or heal a wound. There was regret mixed with those thoughts. Allay tried to ignore the anger that these priests who could cure the drunk and stupid couldn't make her whole.

You are what you are: unique. Kayla thought of Papa and his insistence that Kayla was exactly what she was supposed to be, even though it was hard to keep up with the other kits. "You will just have to find ways to accomplish the same things differently."

Your papa doesn't look like you at all. Allay stood beside Kayla in the memory.

Kayla closed the memory and turned to face the child in reality. It was her own fault for leaving her mind open like that.

How did you do that? The girl was poking at the edges of Kayla's mind.

Don't intrude on another's thoughts when they haven't opened them to you. Kayla gently pushed her mind even farther out of her own. A little distraction with the fish kept the girl from pushing back.

Allay was skilled with a knife for one so young. At that age, Kayla would have reduced the size of the meal to about half what Allay was able to prepare and with her soul knives.

Where did you learn to do that?

The image of a woman in a crude kitchen filled the girl's mind. It was one of the women who raised her. This memory came filled with details such as the woman's name, Cook, and that it had happened nearly five years ago. Kayla followed the memory from the time Cook received a basket of fish at the back door of the kitchen to when Allay slipped into her mind and felt what it was like to fillet a fish.

By all the stars. Kayla pulled herself out of the memory and resisted the urge to pounce on the child. *She doesn't know,* Kayla thought. This time she remembered to keep her thoughts tightly contained, even though the look of anguish on the little demon's face tore at her.

"You have much to learn." Kayla knew the words wouldn't mean anything.

She composed her thoughts as best she could before showing Allay that she shouldn't steal someone else's skill.

It prevents you from learning it for yourself. Kayla let Allay walk with her through the memory of when she'd tried that.

It didn't work for Kayla. Her family all knew to watch out for kits who were frustrated with the learning process. Kayla was no different. The aunt she'd tried to learn from didn't see it that way and came down hard on Kayla.

Allay winced from the memory.

But I can't help it. I see what they think even if I don't try.

Allay hinted at many memories she wished she didn't have. Memories that just happened because she walked by someone who was thinking about it.

I could probably wield a sword, if my arms were strong enough. She thought of all the fights where she knew everything from every perspective.

Don't you know how to shield your mind?

Allay shook her head. *Can you teach me?*

CHAPTER NINE
Allay

Allay watched closely as Kayla showed her how to weave her thoughts around her own mind. There was no way to tell how long they'd been working at this. It looked so easy when Kayla did it. Allay tried, but she left gaps all over the place, and when she opened her eyes, the thoughts dropped away, leaving her as open as she had been before. Only now, she knew what it felt like to have quiet in her mind.

Do it with me. Kayla let her mind fall open.

Allay nodded, keeping her eyes closed so she could concentrate on what she was doing. If she was even capable of doing it. Maybe this kind of thing was something green-skinned people could do, but not a girl like her.

Stop that. Kayla chided. *This wasn't easy for me when I started learning either.*

Allay's eyes snapped open in surprise. *You had to learn?*

Kayla smiled and thought of all the things she'd had to learn that seemed natural now, like walking on just two of her feet. Allay was amazed she'd even bothered when the family she knew was so different from her. That was another surprise, but she didn't dare push that question. She could feel the block Kayla kept around her family memories. Allay would only be able to feel the ones Kayla chose to show her.

Focus. Kayla put the block around Allay's mind for her. *You are as scattered as the rest of them.* Kayla was thinking of the griffins who were still splashing down into the lake but had given up on fishing.

Allay felt herself starting to relax inside the shield when Kayla took it away again. She sighed and closed her eyes, ready to try again to

37

feel that silence for more than two breaths.

Kayla's mind was open now, though her thoughts weren't leaking out. Allay pulled her thoughts together to keep them contained the way Kayla's were.

With a slight brightening of her mind, Kayla began to slowly pull the thoughts around herself. Allay copied her as best she could. It was hard to make thoughts that were only about keeping other people's thoughts out of her head. Allay thought of the quiet she felt when Kayla made the block for her.

That thought was the key. When she focused on the quiet, her thoughts wrapped themselves around her mind easily. She felt the silence edging in with each layer of thoughts that she added to the shield. Kayla matched her pace, letting her see how the thoughts were supposed to overlap, but Allay quit paying attention when the shield was about halfway built. The thoughts of the silence knew where they were needed; it was just a matter of getting them there. At last, the last of the thoughts filled in the last gap and there was complete silence in her mind.

She was alone, for the first time she could remember, with only her own thoughts. She let herself relax slowly into the quiet. Her body released the tension it always held in response to all the thoughts that intruded into her world. She never realized she held her shoulders so tight until just now, when they released as though she were asleep. She wasn't asleep though.

A hand shook her shoulder lightly, then was gone. Allay opened her eyes to the sight of Kayla crouched in that strange stance she'd had when Allay first saw her. Her hands gripped those strange knives of hers. Something crashed through the forest behind her, screaming. Allay jumped to her feet, turning to see Sharl running toward her, beak open and wings folded only as much as necessary.

Kayla yelled something, backing away slowly but keeping her knives in her hands.

"Ah'ee," Sharl cried as she reached them and rose on her hind legs, swiping at Kayla with her claws. "Ah'ee, come."

What are you doing? Allay's thoughts bounced against the inside of her shield. She slid between the angry griffin and the green monster to keep them from killing each other. They were yelling at each other now, neither of them intelligible.

Stop, she wanted to scream at both of them. Her voice still didn't work and all she managed to do was breath a little heavier and make a soft click with her tongue. Neither of which could be heard above the screams. More griffins were coming now. They crashed

38

through the trees above and the bushes below.

"Allay." Kayla pointed to her head when Allay looked around.

Allay shook her head, willing the shield to fall away. It didn't fall like all the others she'd tried had. This time it dispersed like a cloud of steam when Cook lifted the lid of the stew pot.

The world crashed back into her mind. Sharl and the other griffins were bristling with fear for her.

I'm fine. Allay raised her hands to keep Sharl from coming down hard with her claws. *I'm here. I'm fine.*

I thought you were dead. Sharl danced like a horse scared of the barn cat in their little stable behind the inn. *Your mind was gone. The monster...* Sharl imagined all sorts of disgusting things Kayla might have done to her. Allay pushed those thoughts away, wishing she could unthink them.

She was teaching me about the silence. Allay ran a hand down Sharl's neck, forcing the bristled feathers to lie flat again.

Something passed between Sharl and Kayla. Allay turned her mind away, not wanting to know what kinds of insults they would think about each other. She couldn't turn away from the anger and fear that poured out of both. Her shoulders tensed up again; this time they took her stomach with them into that clenched mode.

Stop it. She pushed the thoughts out with a force that made them both take a step back. *I don't want you to hate each other.*

Kayla's thoughts disappeared entirely. Sharl tossed her head and danced from foot to foot, but her thoughts became more peaceful as well. The rest of the griffins pulled back as well. They had found roosts or places to lie among the bushes where they could watch a new story happen.

What do you want? Sharl thought softly.

Allay looked between them. Kayla's knives were hidden again and she stood at her full height. Sharl kept her head high and turned so Kayla was reflected in the middle of her left eye.

I want to help her. Allay focused on Sharl, though she knew Kayla would hear her as well. All the griffins would hear.

The change in the nature of the thoughts around her felt like a wave. Griffins couldn't help it when they saw someone who needed help. That's how she'd become friends with them in the first place. She pushed aside that ugly thought, though it was hard to think of meeting her friends without remembering the men who'd made it possible.

What does she need? So many of them thought it Allay couldn't tell who she heard first.

I want to go home. Kayla's mind projected the way an elder griffin's did when they gathered for storytelling at night. The thought was simple and direct at the same time. It was filled with all the details of what "home" looked like for Kayla.

The griffins clacked their beaks in excitement. *No place like that,* some of them thought, while others wondered how to get there.

The noise gave Allay a headache, until Kayla covered her mind with another shield. This one let her hear and see what people were thinking without it being so overwhelming.

I don't think they can help me. Kayla's thought felt lighter than the others but somehow stronger as well.

They know more than I do, and if they don't know, they'll know who does. Allay had faith in her friends. Griffins knew about the world in ways people just couldn't understand. They lived together, never once thinking they had to do it all on their own. A griffin was always part of a family, lifted and covered just as they were in the heaps they slept in.

Just as she'd predicted, the conversation had turned to names of elders who would know what to do. Quickly, though, the names came with faces and feathers she didn't recognize. They were thinking beyond the flight outside Greylein City. Some names came with a sense of great distance and uncertainty if the one named was still among the living.

Crystal. Sharl thought of the great white dragon who lived high among the snowcapped peaks of the North Mountains.

The rest agreed quickly. *If anyone knows a home like hers, Crystal will know.* They decided quickly, as though thinking up the next game, that Kayla should go to Crystal. With that thought, they indeed began thinking of the next game. In small clumps, the griffins peeled away from the new monster and the human girl to find delight with the wind under their wings.

What is Crystal? Kayla had only a fuzzy image of the great dragon.

Allay couldn't help but think of all the tales of dragons bards had told from the little stage in the corner of the common room at the Broken Ale. She had never met anyone who had seen the dragon who featured in legends and songs older than memory. Allay's own knowledge of the dragon was as fuzzy as the image in Kayla's mind. Crystal was old and wise and a dragon, which made her worthy of fear.

Sharl's feathers bristled out and her tail lashed in response to the fear she felt when thinking of the dragon.

You've never met this Crystal? Kayla asked with a tang of disbelief. She wasn't sure the dragon existed at all, nor that Sharl would suggest a visit to someone she'd never met. *Do you know where she lives?*

Sharl pulled herself up with pride, somehow managing to get just a little taller without lifting her claws from the ground. *Of course I know.* There was an image of a specific peek covered in snow and fog. *Dragons aren't the kind of creatures you just drop in on for a nip of berries.*

We have to take her. Allay put her hand on Sharl's shoulder. *We have to help her get home, even if that means going to the dragon's cave.*

Sharl shook just a little under Allay's hand, but she bowed her head to Allay's thought.

CHAPTER TEN
Kayla

The last time Kayla had sat on another creature's back had been when Papa brought her home from the Krinna village with her claws still fresh. She would have preferred to walk for herself, but her soul was still recovering, which made the effort to keep her balance almost more than she could handle. Papa kept his feet on the ground, except when he had to lift one to move forward. He'd put as much effort into Kayla's balance as she did.

Sitting on Sharl's back while she flew hundreds of feet in the air was an entirely different experience. Kayla had vowed never to allow herself to be so weak that she needed another to walk for her. The ride on Papa had been comfortable, and she'd missed him in the months she'd lived with the Krinna. Sharl promised a nice, smooth ride and that Kayla would be safe, but it would take weeks to walk there and they would have to pass through the capital, where there were even more of the demons/people and some of them would take exception to her skin color. Kayla swore she would never be so desperate as to need to ride a griffin again, out of fear for her life.

You'll get used to it. While Kayla clung to Sharl for her life, Allay delighted in the flight. *There's the Broken Ale.* She leaned over as though trying to dismount while they flew over a small city built in the middle of a prairie.

Kayla couldn't pick out which of the little buildings Allay considered her home. The city itself took all of Kayla's attention. From this height, the people were little more than dots that moved along the narrow alleys that divided the houses from each other. There were small gaps where no buildings rose. Those were filled with canvas-covered booths and even more people. It looked like it would be easier to move around the city on the roofs of the buildings. The thing that really caught her attention was there wasn't a single tree, even a small one, inside the city walls.

Why would you let a tree grow in the city? Allay considered city trees a waste of space and a danger. They could be used to hide all manner of dangerous things.

The trees are *the city.* Kayla imagined Kralt and its trees filled with houses all the way up into the canopy. She'd never been invited into the society that took their place above the streets, not that she wanted to. She'd grown up on the steppe, where everyone except the birds lived on the ground level and there was enough space between families to breathe.

That city below them was a strange mix of the two, taking all the worst of both and shoving them together into a hell deeper than anything she'd seen so far. The allies below were tighter than a bound root system, yet the people pushed through them like ants in an over-crowded colony. She didn't need to ask to know that was where Allay lived. The pull of home showed on the girl's face. As did a hint of guilt.

Your mothers?

Allay clamped down on the thoughts, but they slipped out any-way. She would be late and her mothers would worry. If she was lucky, she'd make it back in time for the gate closing so she would be able to sleep in her own little closet tonight.

Kayla could hope for the same thing. If all went well, this dragon they were going to see would be able to send her home, and she'd be home on the steppe in time to find her place in the sleeping pile of her family.

Sharl flew on, barely noticing her own home in the open space around the city. She headed for the mountains that were just now be-coming visible in the distance. The perspective was off, being so high, but Kayla thought these mountains might be similar to the ones that separated the Steppes of the Felani from the Forests of the Techan. Rocks that rose above the trees on either side. The peaks of these mountains were coated in white too. Her mountains had proven to be a barrier almost stronger than she was for passing between the two countries.

These mountains have too many valleys for that, Sharl mentioned. *The peaks are high, but trade roads cut through every few miles.* Sharl had no respect for the merchants who traveled those roads, though she was able to keep the reasons for her feelings well hidden.

The other thing she saw in Sharl's mind was that the pink demons lived on either side of the mountain. The demons were essential-
ly the same, though the robes they wore had some minor differences.

Don't call them minor to the people, Sharl warned. *But we aren't going
there.*

Sharl thought of the frozen tops of the mountain and a cave
entrance carved in the ice. The image in Sharl's mind suggested the
cave was larger than it needed to be, huge enough to swallow them
whole and not notice. The cave itself had a carnivorous feel in Sharl's
mind.

It approached faster than Kayla would have expected. The
mountains rose out of the ground until she couldn't see the tops. The
rocks and ice were still a fair distance away in front of them. Allay shivered. Kayla felt the cold pouring out from the ice on the mountain.

Do you know where her cave is? Allay asked.

I think so. It shouldn't be too hard to miss. Sharl was flying blind. She
knew what the cave was supposed to look like, but the surrounding
mountains were just a fog of half-remembered thoughts from some
storyteller long ago.

It's just ahead of you. A new voice filled all their minds with the
vision of the cave entrance. The emotions of this image were those of
warmth and home. The cave was in fact just ahead of them, or rather
almost all around them.

*If I'd known you were coming, I would have reduced the illusions for you
sooner.* The mind gave off the sense of being a great hostess and a lover
of good conversation. *I'll have to let you find your own way in. I'm afraid I
haven't been able to turn around in the entrance for some time now. Besides, I need
to get the tea started.*

The mind felt excited in the way only elders could feel. The excitement gave only enough energy to keep the elder from sleeping. Not
like a kit who would be bouncing off everything with the same kind of
anticipation.

The cave Sharl flew into could have held a medium housing
tree from Kralt, with room to spare. Kayla took the measure of the
space and wondered what a creature who couldn't turn around in a
space this large could do with someone as small as her.

Serve you tea, of course. Do you like it with mint or cream?

Kayla was reminded of the old landlady where she lived. All
smiles and cheer, until you didn't pay your rent.

I don't know. I've not had tea here before.

The other mind took a great interest in that. Kayla could feel
it poking through all her surface thoughts, though not trying to get at

anything beyond that. It felt like the meeting between two families at the summer gathers. The only difference was Kayla couldn't follow the mind back to its source and get the same feel off the other.

Oh, child, you have no idea. You'd best land and walk in.

The last felt broader than some of the thoughts that were leaking into her mind. There were images that just couldn't be, so her mind rejected them. There were no such things as snakes with legs and wings. Nor could there ever be a warm-blooded creature who could breathe ice.

Even the power had its limits. It had to work within the realm of possibility. Pulling the heat from something to make it freeze was one thing. Cooling your own breath enough to make something else freeze within it was dangerous at best.

Sharl landed on a smooth, flat rock. It looked almost as white as snow, except for thin veins of pink that ran through it. Overhead, it was hard to see the ceiling. Kayla slid off Sharl's back, landing in a defensive crouch, though she had no idea what she might need to defend against. The mind that had touched hers held no malice or predatory thoughts.

Deep breaths and thoughts of tea usually help my visitor.

Kayla couldn't help but think that she didn't know what tea was.

I can't give you that. You'll just have to come experience for yourself.

Sharl, Allay, and Kayla glanced at each other, each making eye contact with the other two before moving farther into the cave. The air was as chilled as Kayla would expect at the top of a mountain, with a warm feeling too. Her dress did nothing to keep the chill from cooling her blood. She pushed through her stiffening muscles, willing herself to warm up with the movement. By the time they'd walked the length of the cave and found the much larger chamber this entryway led to, she felt almost normal.

The sight of a cavern lit by starlight and filled with clouds stopped her in her tracks. Allay and Sharl stopped beside her. They were each leaking fear and fascination.

Come in, come in. A bit of the clouds rolled away, revealing a small table with three places set. Two were typical plates and cups with golden utensils at the side of the plates. The third held a large shallow bowl. It looked like just the kind of thing a griffin would find easier to drink from. In the center of the table were three teapots with different shapes and sizes. One was made from copper but was the most exquisite, shaped like a flower. Kayla almost recognized the design, but it was just a little different than anything she could name.

I always wondered why that pot came to me. It had to be for some guest I would entertain. You are the first to make it feel just right.

It's beautiful. I never would have guessed copper for a decorative.

A physical voice from high above chuckled. Words came down as well that made Allay smile, though Kayla couldn't catch the meaning.

Oh, dear me, you really are from a long way off, aren't you?

A giant creature descended from the clouds overhead. Except it wasn't the whole creature, only a head with a snout like an alligator and ears like a gazelle. The eyes were set too far forward to be a heard beast and too far back to be a predator. The head was attached to a snakelike neck that curved off into the cloudbank. It dropped all the way down until the chin rested on the stone floor, and Kayla still had to look up to the eyes. The predator's pointed teeth however were right at eye height.

Will you allow me to fix your minor language issue?

"What issue?" Kayla found herself in her defensive crouch again, this time with claws drawn.

The one that keeps you from using your voice effectively here. Those sounds are going to frighten your companions if you use them too much.

Kayla glanced at Allay, who had backed up against Sharl. Sharl's feathers were ruffled and her eyes were fixed on Kayla.

What do you want to do?

The lips she stood next to tightened, then pulled up in what must have been a grin. *Give you the language she understands.*

Kayla nodded, though she didn't lose her stance. She couldn't understand why she was so jumpy all of a sudden. The stars knew she had more to fear from the pink demons who had attacked her earlier. There was more to fear from falling off the back of a griffin who could easily forget she was carrying anyone.

She felt the mind of the dragon slide into her own. It carried tendrils of thoughts with it and sent them into every part of her memory. These thoughts weren't complete and they sought matches within her own mind. Words formed when they found her own thoughts that matched. Kayla thought about things in sequences that didn't make sense: lake, fountain, gazelle, home, Krinna, tree, home tree, flight, etc.

The thoughts and words came faster and faster, until she couldn't separate them anymore.

CHAPTER ELEVEN
Lord Corawin Tromadin

"Sir." One of the dog handlers approached with his dog at heal. "We have news."

Corawin glared at the man, daring him to say anything that would put him in a worse mood. "Unless you've found the demon, be careful what you say."

The man stopped farther from him than was dictated by rank. "A local saw a fire on that island yesterday. We've commandeered his boat to investigate."

"Is that all?"

"He…" The man took a half step back. "He said there was a flight of griffins here at about that time. He thinks they may—"

"Griffins don't use fire." Any idiot would know that.

Griffins were glorified hawks that weren't smart enough to be trained to the hunt. They were more of a nuisance than any other pest.

It had taken two days of searching to realize that creature had come this far through that blue hole she was so fond of throwing around. Two days and they just now found she might have been here as long as yesterday. He stayed his hand from flipping the knife he was holding into the man's chest.

"Well, get on with it."

"Yes, sir." He bowed himself away, though he didn't take his eyes off the knife. Corawin let the breach of etiquette go for now, though he would keep an eye on that one. A proper bow lowered the eyes all the way. You must show your lord that you trust him.

"Sir?" Brace approached with an impeccable bow. "Have you

considered your orders if we don't find her here?"

Corawin scowled, but he couldn't dismiss his best tracker and most loyal subject so easily.

"What are you suggesting?"

Brace stood to his full height. "If I may speak freely?"

Corawin waved for him to do so.

"You requested a hero, someone with a specific skill set. One of those skills was the ability to get into the palace and close to the royals. She is showing exactly that kind of skill. She has ways to slip past even the best tracker."

"You mean you can't track her."

"Sir." He nodded. "Nor can any of the dogs who are by far better trackers than I."

Brace always could make a believable show of humility, one of the traits that had allowed him to rise so fast. It also kept him at a level below his skill. Brace could have been a commander in Corawin's personal guard, if he'd ever bothered to try for it.

"What's your point?"

"It took us this long to find her here, and she has been here since she slipped our perimeter. Time for her to heal and regain her strength. There is no telling where she might run off to."

The knife that had been in his hand was now embedded in a tree fifty feet behind Brace. Corawin hated to admit it, but his man had a point.

"If she's on that island, we'll take her and bind her any way we can."

Brace nodded.

"And if she's not, you'll lead a team to find and kill her." Truth was she'd already proven herself to be more of a liability than an asset. He couldn't let this situation deteriorate any further.

"Sir?"

"Was I unclear?"

"You want us to kill the demon you just summoned."

"So you did hear me." He struggled to keep his voice even. All the more galling because Brace had no blood worth respecting. What he had were skills Corawin couldn't find in a better man.

"Sir, this may not be the wisest path."

Corawin flipped the knife he held. "Go on."

Brace let a grin touch his lips briefly. "She's behaving like the fox in a fox hunt. If the hounds get too aggressive, they can end up dead."

"Then you'd best not get too aggressive." Corawin waved him

away.

"We'll need a special hunting permit." Brace bowed and continued to explain without waiting for a request or permission. "She is already at the borders of your land. Chances are we'll have to follow her all over the country. I wouldn't want my team to bring undue political pressures by trespassing."

"Damn it all." Corawin stomped an unsuspecting blade of grass into oblivion. "I'll secure the damned permit." If he believed the gods actually cared, he'd swear they were laughing at him. All of them up there laughing and taking turns to see who could make this situation worse.

Getting that kind of permit was always politically dicey. He couldn't just tell the king he needed a special permit to hunt the demon he'd summoned to kill the king. That was a good way to end up in the dungeons as a traitor. He'd have to come up with a good enough cover story. Vague enough to allow His Majesty to fill in the blanks on his own and scary enough to hurry the process.

"With your permission, I'll begin selecting my team and making preparations." Brace bowed again. "You know, she's probably sick, considering the color of her skin." Then he turned and left without waiting for Corawin to dismiss him.

He threw a second knife over Brace's head. The man was too valuable to threaten directly, but he couldn't be allowed to take too many liberties.

"Pack up," he ordered his valet.

It didn't matter what they found on that island. Either the demon was there and they'd take her or she wasn't and they'd fall all over themselves to assure him they would find her. Either way, he needed to head to the capital to head off the scandals this episode would generate.

CHAPTER TWELVE
Allay

Dragons are scary. Allay knew that from all the stories and songs the bards who came to the Broken Ale told. According to those same stories and songs, dragon caves were supposed to be huge spaces filled with a great mound of gold in the middle and the bones and armor of the brave knights who had failed to kill the dragon in residence. They also said that dragons were supposed to defend their hoards with tooth, tail, and magic.

Crystal fit only one of those. She was scary, but only because her teeth were taller than Allay. Her cave did have a lot of gold in it, displayed on shelves that reached all the way to the ceiling. The ceiling, when Allay caught a glimpse of it through the clouds, was higher than the tallest spires dedicated to Irdra, goddess of the stars. There were no bones or battered bits of armor scattered about. In fact, the cave was as well lit and clean as she imagined the palace would be. Best of all, Crystal served the lightest, flakiest, sweetest pastries with wild berry jam baked inside.

Kayla didn't seem to notice any of it. She stood as still as a statue, staring into Crystal's eye. Her mind was blank, or blocked, so there was nothing she could do about it. The dragon had pulled something from Allay's mind earlier—she said it was language, but Allay felt her touch just about every memory she had—then had gone as silent as Kayla.

This is going to make the best story. Sharl pranced around the cave, poking her beak into everything without actually touching anything.

No one will believe you. Allay projected all the stories she'd heard about dragons and how they were supposed to behave.

Silly humans. Sharl went on poking about the cave. *Griffins know truth when they feel it.*

Allay laughed. It was a common theme between them, how much better griffins were than humans. Most of the time, Allay had to agree.

Oh nonsense, Crystal's thoughts interrupted. *Humans have their good points too.* She thought of the villages all around the mountains who put out elder animals where it was easier to catch them. *Griffins aren't organized enough to herd animals for food.*

Sharl fluffed her feathers, but accepted the jibe with her usual good humor. *And there would be no Allay without the humans.*

Sharl, would you be so good as to hunt up some live rabbits? I'm afraid I haven't been able to catch a rabbit for some time.

The image of the huge dragon trying to pounce on a tiny rabbit made Allay giggle.

Sharl wondered about the "live" part, but Crystal insisted on it. The griffin took it as a challenge as she bolted for the door.

Now, let's see what we can do for you. Crystal's mind loomed as large as her body in Allay's mind.

Allay shrank away from the dragon, though she had so many questions.

Your friend is fine, just far from home.

Allay looked to where Kayla had sunk to the floor with her legs folded beneath her. Her back was straight, but her eyes were closed now. A thin line of golden light coiled around her, twisting and turning over her whole body.

What's happening? Allay couldn't connect the warm, comforting emotions with the horrible image she was seeing.

It is her magic. Crystal pulled Allay's attention back to her own mind. *There isn't much here, but for her, it is as vital as food.*

Crystal let her see more than Kayla had about the desperate position Kayla was in. The strange woman was starving in more ways than one. The hedgelock berries she had eaten, the ones that could have killed anyone else, didn't hurt her, but didn't nourish her either. That light wrapping itself around her did more than power her magic; it could keep her alive in the absence of food.

Magic can do that?

Hers can. Crystal pulled Allay into her mind and let her see all the magics of the world. Colored threads of light twisted around everything. So many different colors it was amazing they didn't blend into a muddy mess. Some of them reached out toward her but slipped back to

54

where they came from before they touched her.

There are so many colors. Do painters know about all these colors? She'd seen some of the painters mixing colors on the little boards they balanced on one hand. No painting had so many colors as she saw in Crystal's mind though.

I'm sure they do.

The priests can see this? What do they do with so many colors? She imagined the priests like painters, creating magic with all the colors by painting it onto the world.

Why the magic won't touch you is a mystery. You have more than enough imagination. Crystal laughed a deep rumbling sound that shook Allay all the way through to her heart. *This is what dragons see. Humans are more limited.*

The view changed until only the reddish-orange of bad metal flowed through the world. These lines never once reached toward her. They covered everything, flowing in and out of the rocks as easily as they moved about the cave. They didn't quite cover everything. Kayla and about a foot of space around her were empty except for one thread that twisted around her but never quite touched her.

It won't touch her either.

She isn't part of this world.

Allay watched through Crystal's eyes as her own body filled with the red lines of power.

Why?

There was no answer, like Crystal's mind had gone blank.

Allay slid back into her own mind, where her memories of Kayla waited for her. Kayla's mind, like Crystal's, was open and closed at the same time. There were thoughts she could see and some she couldn't. Kayla had shared memories of her home, where the colors were all different. The grass where her heart lived was red like the lines of power here. The people were green like her and the trees reached up into a yellow sky.

Where do these things come from? Allay pushed the memories toward Crystal.

If I knew that, I would take her there.

That surprised Allay. Adults seemed to know everything, and they were only a couple of decades. A dragon of Crystal's size was hundreds of years old. She had to know just about everything there was to know.

About three thousand. Crystal made Allay understand just how long that was. *I was hatched before Greylein existed as a nation. I've seen your whole history, yet I still learn something interesting every day.*

Sharl soared through the cave entrance then. *I got two. Had three, but one escaped. Why did you want them alive?*

Because I can't convert them if they are dead. Crystal lifted her head to take the rabbits. *Allay, I'll need your help for this next part. Climb up and get the small glass phial.*

Allay could see exactly where and how to get what Crystal wanted and why Crystal couldn't get it for herself. The little cubby had become too small for her to use. Allay, however could have climbed all the way inside if she needed to. She didn't need to; the phial, which was bigger than any Allay had ever seen, even in the herbalist's shop, was close to the front. She tucked it into the top of her bodice for the climb back down.

Kayla looked a bit more vibrant when Allay returned. *What happened?*

I found some power. Kayla grinned as she let Allay feel the difference.

Enough of that, Crystal chided. *You need so much more than a little trickle of power.*

A thick blanket of truth fell over them both. Allay tried to understand the sudden shift in Crystal's mind.

Kayla let her face return to neutral. *I need to go home.*

Which I can't do for you. Best I can do is keep you from dying. Crystal had one of the rabbits suspended in the air over Kayla. *I need some of your blood.*

Allay looked up at the dragon, questioning the vision of herself collecting the green liquid in the phial she still had in her bodice. Kayla only nodded. One of her knives appeared in her hand and slid neatly across her other arm. The knife was gone as though it had never been there by the time Allay got the phial under the wound to catch the blood. It really was green.

Very good. Crystal pulled Allay into her vision again. *I'll need your hands, if you don't mind.*

Allay accepted Crystal into her mind as well. The feeling of the dragon manipulating her hands gave Allay a bit of a thrill. The side effect was that she could see with the dragon's magic vision again, which showed several colors of power twining around a single drop of the green blood that was laced with the golden lines as well.

Then the rabbit came into view as well. Allay could see its fear fogging the air around it. Poor creature. The rabbit was laced with red lines with a few green and yellow ones too. Crystal pulled the golden lines from the blood and covered some of the red lines with them. The golden lines moved along the red lines, covering them until all the red had become gold and the rabbit was dead.

She felt the weight of the rabbit in her hands as Crystal retreated to her own mind, leaving only the impression that Allay should cook it as blandly as she could. Allay found a small hearth with a cheery fire in it where a bank of fog had been.

Sharl pestered her all through dinner preparations about what was going on. Allay couldn't explain or even think clearly about what she'd experienced. She brought the rabbit out for Kayla and found a fully set table, complete with a roasted rabbit for her and Sharl to share. Kayla set a bowl of salad greens on the table.

Allay smiled. Crystal had many strange ways about her. This was the best adventure she'd ever had. If only she could tell Missy and Cook about this.

CHAPTER THIRTEEN
Lord Corawin Tromadin

Corawin rode hard for the capital. In the last leg, he let his personal guard fall behind. He left a small contingent in the city at all times. He could gather them before anyone realized there would be an opportunity. Or so he had thought. He didn't expect the city guard would be the first issue he'd have to face.

He was a lord of the council. Silly rules like gate closing shouldn't apply to him.

"Sorry, Lord." The guard with the most bangles on his uniform bowed halfway to him. "Once the gates are closed, we cannot open them until morning."

"Nonsense." Corawin glared down at the man who should have understood he was in danger of his life with nonsense like this. "If you can open them with the sun, you can open them now."

The man bowed less than halfway this time. "The keys for the great locks aren't kept in the guard houses, sire. That would be a silly failure of our security. The marshal will bring the keys in the morning." A third bow that barely made it a quarter of the way. "I can allow you to enter through the guard's way, if you don't mind leaving your horse."

What nerve. "I cannot walk through the city." Of all the stupid ideas he'd heard from the lower classes.

"I am sorry, but your horse simply will not fit through the side door." The guard didn't even attempt to bow this time.

Corawin glanced back to the dust cloud his guards were making, realizing how stupid it was to have left them behind. He could wait for them and said so to the guard captain. Not that the man paid proper attention. And they still wouldn't be allowed to bring their horses through the gate. Worse than that, they were forced to walk bent in half through the guard's gate until they reached the main room of the guard tower. That was overcrowded with men who should learn to bathe more often and had even less tact than the captain.

He fumed about such horrible treatment all the way to the palace gate, which was also closed and guarded.

"Let me through. I have urgent business with his Royal Majesty."

The guards thrust their halberds out to form a cross between them, blocking Corawin from the gate.

"Do you know who I am?" Corawin drew himself up as far as his stature would allow.

Without moving, the two men answered in chorus, "Lord Corawin Tromadin, fifth seat on the council of lords."

"Your lordship." Sir Delare, the king's own, stood on the other side of the gate. "These men do not have the authority to open this gate for you or anyone, including his Royal Majesty himself. They will open again tomorrow after second bells."

Corawin had never heard of the palace gates being closed to all. Closed of course during sensitive negotiations when a disturbance could tip the balance away from a fair deal. Council members were always informed of such dealings and were exempt from the ban.

"Under whose authority?"

Delare bowed as deep as anyone could expect, yet there was a feeling of sarcasm to it that rankled. "Mine as the king's own. It was decided just yesterday, so I suspect the missive missed you on your way here." He stood again with a smile. "His Royal Majesty is meeting with the delegation from Trevalain. It is a delicate negotiation."

"So delicate the council isn't involved?"

Corawin swallowed his anger. No need to show emotion to a man who had the right and responsibility to say anything to the king.

"And if there is an emergency?" Corawin asked with a smile to match his.

"That is why I am here." He gestured to the ground below his feet. "Tell me of this emergency."

Corawin looked pointedly at the two guards who were doing their best impression of statues. "It's the kind that requires some discretion."

"Ah." The king's own nodded. "Then we can move this discussion to the servants' gate." He waved off to the left.

The servants' gate was often left unguarded—everyone knew

that. It was protected my mechanical means, which caught any number of would-be thieves and assassins every year. It also occasionally killed a careless servant. Corawin glanced in that direction. It would take him into a poorly lit ally intended for servants.

"Or you could just wait until tomorrow morning." The king's own grinned like a man who knew he'd won at a game of chess. "I'll be sure his majesty is ready for you at second bells."

Corawin scowled. "I'll see you at the servants' gate."

The servants' gate was little more than a door made of iron bars set into the wall in a small indent of the palace wall. Half the citizens of the city wouldn't know where to find the servants gate even though they'd probably walked past it at least once per week. Corawin would have preferred not to know of it, but his duty as a council member required him to "investigate" the deaths that occurred when the mechanism did its job. From the outside, the deadly gears and levers were completely concealed. It made him that much less comfortable to be standing near the gate, waiting for a man he barely trusted to pass judgment on his problem.

"Lord Tromadin, I suggest you keep back at bit." Delare was waiting for them. Of course, the route inside would be shorter. "We can speak freely here without fear of being overheard."

"So you say, yet anyone could be just out of sight." He squared himself to the gate and held the other man's eyes in a challenge.

The king's own smiled and nodded. "As you say, so it is. I can only ask you to trust me."

"And if I don't?"

"I'll see you tomorrow at second bells."

Corawin scowled but told the man about the sick woman who had gone crazy and fled from one of his villages.

"This would be the green-skinned woman?"

How in all the heavens did he know about that?

"We believe she is a danger. My men are prepared to track her."

"So you want a special hunting permit to allow you access to other lands."

Was he a mind reader? Corawin struggled to keep his composure. "You've guessed it."

"I'll have it delivered to your home before first bells." He bowed and turned to walk away.

"Wait." Corwin stopped himself from stepping forward.

"Sir?"

Corawin wanted to ask how he'd known or why all the theatrics, but that would make him look weak. "Tell His Majesty I am grateful."

"Of course, sir." He bent in another deep bow. "Just be sure you take care of this mess discreetly."

Corawin held his stance until the man was out of sight. When he was sure he was alone, with only his own men, he let his temper flare. He ranted all the way to his city estate about the pompousness of a man from unknown origins who had somehow managed to get appointed to an official position. And he never did hear what was going on between the king and a delegation from Trevelain. They weren't a usual ally nor an enemy worth watching too closely.

CHAPTER FOURTEEN
Kayla

Time in the ice cave flowed in odd ways. At once, Kayla felt as though she'd been still too long and that they had just arrived. The new language felt strange in her mouth, and being able to speak it did her no good in this company. She would need to meet other people to practice and to learn more about why she had been brought here.

How are you feeling? Crystal was still hidden in the mists that were a perpetual illusion in the cave. They had been in existence for so long the spell no longer needed constant maintenance.

More like myself. Kayla admitted. Her reserves of power were nearly full. The changed rabbit Crystal made for her kept her well fed, even if it tasted tainted. She hadn't gotten sick from them yet, and it was better than chewing randomly on leaves and berries. *We should probably leave soon. I don't want to cause you any trouble.*

Crystal's head emerged from the bank of clouds high above Kayla and dropped until her eyes were almost head level. *You've been great guests. I will miss your company.*

Kayla laid a hand on the dragon's nose. *You will not like the demons who are chasing me.*

Crystal twitched with laughter. *They are men, not demons.*

Kayla imagined little demons inside the men. *They pulled me from my world and my mate. I don't care what species they may have been born. They are demons.*

Crystal agreed with her. *Yet you must deal with them, specifically the lord at their lead.* Crystal showed her an image of the red lines wrapped all around her, with a small tail leading to the fancy one's chest. *That spell holds you here. There is nothing that can send you home while it is still wrapped around you.*

Kayla looked down with her own eyes, knowing she would see nothing. Simply knowing about the various powers didn't give her eyes that could see them.

"How do I remove them?"

Allay and Sharl looked up from the game they were playing with sticks and little rocks.

"You do not. Only that man has the power to remove them. When he decides you have done what he wanted you to do, they will unravel. Or maybe they will reverse your travels and send you home. That part is hard to read."

Kayla understood. Knowing what another had done with power was tricky when you knew the customs and beliefs of the caster.

You should just ask him and do it. Allay's thought was laced with loneliness.

Then I would have to leave you all alone. Kayla smiled at the child.

I'm not alone! Allay imagined the griffin pile she slept in on nights she was out of the city.

Kayla thought back about the other shop children who didn't share their games with her. *You are getting stronger, but it will take more than strength of mind to be accepted by your peers.*

Allay's face became a mask of neutrality.

Child! Crystal's head lifted above them all. Her tail slapped the ground, stirring a wind that chased the fog through the cave. *You have a family that is waiting for you? Why have you not thought of them before now?*

Allay shrank away from the dragon, making herself as small as possible.

Sharl puffed her feathers and backed away.

Kayla's mind was filled with images of two women. Crystal's version had them disheveled, sleep deprived, and crying their eyes out while Allay's had them working efficiently, serving lecherous men while managing to keep themselves just out of arm's reach.

"Your mothers love you." Kayla spoke to avoid the power struggle in their minds. "We should get you home before they lose any more sanity than they already have."

Allay's eyes went wide. *They aren't insane.*

Any mother who doesn't know where her child is loses sanity. Kayla thought of her own mother when her sister was out on walkabout. Even though it was a normal and expected part of life, Mother couldn't sleep more than a few hours at a time. Her hunting skills suffered. She kept Kayla closer than she ever had before. No doubt she was doing

64

the same now that Kayla was on walkabout. She'd already been gone three years. How much longer would Mother suffer now?

I didn't mean it. Allay was near tears now.

Never the less, it's time to get you home. Crystal pulled the anger from her thoughts. *Sharl, help me gather a few things.*

The ever-present fog condensed into the peak at the top of the cave, revealing walls of little grottoes and a few larger shelves all filled with a strange collection of things. Kayla couldn't see the organization in it, but Crystal guided Sharl to each piece she needed.

Crystal's full body was also visible for the first time since they had arrived. Kayla took the time to admire the sleek form that was wound around the edges of the cave. Her neck and tail were almost snakelike. She could bend each of them into a twisted knot and untie it without apparent pain or difficulty. In the middle, she bulked out though kept the sleek physique of a bird. Her wings were folded over her back and her four short legs barely held her off the floor.

The wings held Kayla's attention. They appeared to be webbed with a shimmery material she'd seen in Kralt that would reflect different colors depending on the angle of the light but had little structural strength. Women liked to cover dresses with the stuff when they dressed up for the evening. Such dresses weren't meant to be worn more than once.

My wings are more than strong enough to hold me. Crystal stretched one out into the middle of the cave. It had the same rainbow effect as the material from Kralt but sounded more like the leathery wings of a Turatura bird.

They are beautiful

Thank you. Now I have some things for you.

The first was a leather satchel with a wide strap that fit comfortably over Kayla's shoulder. Next a copper bowl that would make it easier for Kayla to gather her power. A tin of spice to make the vegetables more palatable.

Don't let anyone else touch it, though.

She also had a pouch filled with smoked change-rabbit.

This won't last long. I expect you to come visit as often as you need to.

I would prefer to provide for myself.

Crystal laughed. *If I could teach you that, I would, but I don't know if your power can make this transformation, and even if it could, you would spend more than you regain making change-rabbits for yourself.*

Kayla knew she was right, but the spice was something she would be able to mix for herself, and she could live on vegetables longer than Crystal imagined. Not that she would stay away just because she wanted to be independent. Good friends were rare in any world.

I don't have much in the way of appropriate clothing for you, but this cloak will conceal you until you can acquire something better.

Kayla took the cloak from Sharl. It almost reached her ankles but could have wrapped around her body several times.

I took it off a silly knight who came for my treasure, many years ago. I doubt his great grandchildren will recognize the cloak.

You killed him? Allay broke in with shock.

Not until he jammed that damned sword into my knee. In the memory she shared, Crystal had been more than patient with a man covered in flats of metal with fabric draped over the outside. How he thought he could fight in a getup like that? The best fighters were the ones who weren't where you thought they were. It was hard enough to move like that with the dress she was wearing. Covered in metal would be even harder, not to mention you would have no chance to sneak up on your prey.

Off you go, then. Crystal let the fog fall back into place leaving only a clear path to the entryway. *Sharl, you get that child home as fast as you can. Break the rules.*

Sharl waited only long enough for Kayla and Allay to climb up before wrapping them in the invisible force that kept them on her back. She was airborne a breath later and out over the snow-covered slopes.

Kayla was ready for the erratic flight of a griffin this time, now that she knew Sharl had enough power to keep her in place through everything. She could enjoy the views, watching the ground shift and change below them.

Those men must be surprised. Allay giggled at the image of several men with other beasts looking up at them from a ledge just below the snow pack on the mountain. *Crystal keeps the entrance hidden.*

Kayla was more worried about the markings on their armor that were just like the ones she saw in that cave where she first arrived. Maybe she hadn't moved soon enough to save Crystal from her troubles.

CHAPTER FIFTEEN
Lord Corawin Tromadin

Sir Delare had been as good as his word. The scroll granting him and his men the right to range over other lord's lands in pursuit of the green demon arrived before even the kitchen fires had been lit.

Corawin would have been in his saddle and on his way to meet Brace and the rest of the hunting parties immediately. However, other lords heard of this in time to be at his door, seeking an explanation before the breakfast bread had cooled enough to slice. It took him the whole day to assure them all that "there is nothing to worry about, I have it all under control" without explaining exactly what was going on.

That kind of dithering nonsense was exactly the reason the country was in the state it was. Making treaties and alliances that were going to cost them to maintain rather than demanding the respect that came with military strength. Too many of the lords currently on the council were more worried about keeping up production than building the strength of the nation. Their weakness would be shown to the world if His Royal Majesty King Thorwin were allowed to go through with his plan to name his daughter, Silvanie, heir to the throne.

A woman king, what a laughing stock. All those treaties and alliances could be thrown right out with the chamber pot if she were to take the throne. How could they not see the coming disaster?

All those lords, coming one after another, each expecting him to receive them as a gracious host to discuss the matter of the kind of respect they would expect from his men when they entered their territory. They expected his household staff to have tea and sweat breads ready for them to consume. His staff hadn't even been prepared for his arrival. What irritated him more was he had to cater to them because he still needed their support. At least until he salvaged this plan and got that demon to understand what she had been brought over to do.

Sir Delare must have arranged all this; it was just his style. Corawin had never approved of his appointment, nor the tasks to which he was assigned. The king's own was supposed to be the one who could speak for the king in any situation and advise him when no others could or would. What a silly notion. Most of the time, Sir Delare walked among the peasants, acting like he was one of them. He heard their petty disputes. Ate at their tables. He even distributed his special coins to make the lowly feel important.

When he gained the throne, Corawin wouldn't have a king's own. He had the council for bad advice if he needed it. What did the peasants need with hope that could never be realized? They would be better off keeping their minds on the mud where they belonged. Leave the worries to those born to such power.

All that took time. A day to be exact. A day that did allow his men to get the horses into the city and properly curried. Also a day delayed in finding Brace and his crew. Brace was wise enough to continue the hunt even without the proper papers. When Corawin found them, their camp looked like any brigand's fire.

"You can wear your colors again," Corawin announced as he dropped out of the saddle. "What have you learned?"

The men bowed where they stood around the fire.

"A single griffin matching the colors of the one seen leaving Lake Thorn has been spotted hunting more rabbits than one griffin should eat." Brace didn't raise his eyes to meet Corawin's.

"I don't give a rat's tail about the damned griffin."

"Of course not, sir." He kept his eyes down, though he raised his chin a bit. "There are caves above the snow line here. We believe she is hiding in one of them and using the griffin to do her hunting and perhaps scouting."

Corawin sighed. "How can anyone use a griffin as a scout?" Corawin removed his riding gloves and slapped them against his leg. "Have you gone daft?"

"Sir." Brace bowed again. "She is a demon with powers we've never seen before. It's not so much of a stretch to think she could take over the creature's mind and see through its eyes the way a witch uses a raven."

Damn, that would complicate things. If she could take control of a griffin, there would be no reason for her to touch the ground at all, which would put even Brace's tracking skills to the test.

68

"What makes you think she's up there?" Corawin pointed up toward the mountain just in time to see a griffin appear from a glacier, already in flight. It did look like the griffin they'd seen fly away from Lake Thorn.

There were shapes that didn't belong to a griffin attached to it. He was as sure as if he'd seen her eyes that it was the demon on his back. She'd grown in her time here. Or so it would appear.

The griffin took a lazy turn just over them, showing the demon clearly and a child riding on the griffin's back.

This could only get worse if they were to wing their way back to the capital. Which was exactly the direction they were flying.

"Mount up and follow them," Corawin ordered, jumping into his own saddle. Even riding as hard as he could, the horse was no match for the speed of a griffin in the air. They were out of sight within ten minutes, though their course was clear.

"By the light of dark!" Corawin screamed into the distance.

The men kept back as his horse reared in response to his anger.

"Sir." Brace pulled his horse closer to him than the others. "This may be exactly what you want. She's heading to the capital. Perhaps she'll—"

"Don't say it."

CHAPTER SIXTEEN
Allay

Sharl flew high all the way from the mountains to the city. She kept her thoughts to herself, though there was a darkness to the silence Allay couldn't understand. Instead, she tried to enjoy the scenery, though from this high there wasn't much to see, just a mash of colors making interesting patterns in the countryside.

Kayla's mind was just as shrouded, though her silence made more sense. Allay had glimpsed a bit of the fear Kayla felt about the city. To her, people were something strange and fearful. Funny that, most people would think the same of her. In stories, green skin meant you were a monster. That was all she'd seen before Kayla tightened her grip on her thoughts.

Hold tight. Sharl imagined a fall from the sky right into the back court of the Broken Ale.

Allay didn't have to imagine it. Sharl folded her wings and bent her head toward the ground. The city started as just a patch of brown but grew quickly to reveal the walls and streets of the city in a way Allay had never imagined. It wasn't hard to see the differences between the lords and the rest of the people like this. Allay opened her mouth to scream, but as usual, nothing but her breath escaped.

Just as well, the guards on the city wall would hear her and try to shoot Sharl out of the sky. Griffins weren't allowed inside the city. They were wild animals who had no place among civilization. So said the guards. Allay would love to tell them how sophisticated the griffins could be. If they were so dangerous, why were they allowed to live in the plains outside the city walls? Allay didn't understand and, for the moment, didn't really care.

She recognized the yard of the Broken Ale a few heartbeats before Sharl snapped her wings open and pulled up to land lightly in the yard.

"No, go away." Cook came out flapping a towel at them. "We don't need anymore wood. Oh!"

Missy came out a moment later with two towels in her hands. She stopped short, her mouth open and eyes wide.

Your mothers? Kayla matched the women standing open-mouthed and frozen in front of them to the images she'd shared.

Allay nodded.

Well, go greet them. Kayla nudged her off Sharl's back.

Allay slid to the ground, her heart still pounding from the thrill of the drop out of the sky. Her feet forgot how to walk for the first few steps. Then she was within arm's reach of Cook, who reached out and pulled her away from the griffin.

"Get away from us." Cook brandished the towel at Sharl and Kayla.

Missy wrapped her arms around Allay so tight it was hard to breath.

"Oh, sweetie, what happened? We were so worried."

Concentrate. Kayla reminded her of the drills she and Crystal had led her through to strengthen her mind and keep the unwanted thoughts out. They had also suggested the same discipline could be used to reach her thoughts into the minds of other people.

She closed her eyes to help concentrate. *I'm fine.*

"You, get out of here." Cook flapped the towel at Sharl again. "And take that with you."

Something a little more direct, Sharl suggested.

I love you.

Missy grabbed her shoulders and pushed her back just a bit. "What did you say?"

Allay looked into Missy's eyes, feeling all the love and concern she was feeling.

I love you.

Then there was fear. "What happened to you?" Missy didn't let go, but she held Allay at arm's distance.

"What's wrong?" Cook asked.

"I thought she talked, but… It wasn't her."

I can talk, just not with my voice. This time she concentrated on Cook.

Cook stumbled back.

"Mistress, there is nothing wrong with your daughter." Kayla slid down from Sharl's back.

Missy pushed Allay behind her now, stepping between her and Kayla the way she did when the drunks got ugly ideas.

This is Kayla, my friend. Allay tried to push the idea that Kayla was harmless, but her teeth and skin didn't help.

"Stay back." Cook had a knife in her hand now.

"Please be calm." Kayla's voice sounded strange. She held out her hands, empty, and palms up to prove she wasn't a danger, just like men who didn't want to fight in the pub. "Please be calm."

Are you magicking them? Allay slipped around Missy to confront Kayla.

Kayla let her feel the same feeling she pressed into Missy and Cook. *They are free to think their own thoughts.*

There was a sense of calm flowing through all her thoughts. Even knowing it came from Kayla, it was hard to ignore. Her heart slowed and breathing became even.

Missy, Cook. This is my friend, Kayla. Allay took their hands and pulled them forward to meet her new friend.

"Hello." Missy let go of Allay's hand and reached out to shake Kayla's.

"Hello." Kayla bowed slightly over Missy's hand. "It is a pleasure to meet you."

"And you." Cook took her turn shaking Kayla's hand.

"Please, come in." Missy smiled and waved to the kitchen door.

Allay let out a breath. Then she smiled at Kayla. *This is my family.*

Kayla smiled back. "I've heard so much about you. It's nice to meet you in person." She followed Missy's hand toward the kitchen door.

"Can we get you anything to eat?" Cook asked, following close behind.

Well, that went better than expected, Sharl commented.

Allay nodded. *You'd better get out of here before those guards figure out where you landed.*

Sharl didn't wait to think about the consequences of being caught in the city. Most people thought her no more than an animal. She pushed herself skyward almost as fast as she had fallen, rising out of the range of the guards on the city wall before they noticed she was there.

Allay watched her go. She'd never thought to have one of her griffin friends in the yard. How much else had changed in the last few days? The best thing was she'd been able to tell her mothers she loved them.

Not enough. The sound of armor clanking and boots slapping against the street told her the guards had figured out where Sharl had landed.

Guards. She projected to Kayla as she ran for the kitchen door.

"Can you hide me?" Kayla wasn't smiling anymore.

"Of course." Missy stood from the small table in the nook.

"Why?" Cook stood by the end of the table, blocking Kayla into her seat.

Guards. Allay tugged Cook away.

They were all action then. Missy pulling Kayla into the pantry while Cook jumped into the work of a kitchen. Allay had seen this before and knew her role in the play.

She pulled a clean apron over her dress that showed a little too much of her adventures and headed for the common room just in time for the city guards to pour through the front door. Half the customers ran for the back door but were stopped by guards coming in that way.

"Everyone stay where you are," the guard captain ordered in a loud voice.

He wasn't a man Allay had met before, so he wouldn't know she was mute. She could make him believe her deaf too.

"Girl, where's the barkeep?"

Allay just stared at him.

"She don't never talk," one of the regular drunks called.

"Go get the barkeep." The captain stepped forward.

Allay cowered away from him but stayed in the doorway to give Missy and Cook as much time as possible. She'd gotten really good at this.

"Go on, girl." He waved at her.

Allay shrank even farther, letting tears form in her eyes. She could feel his frustration rising and with it the thought of finally catching the griffin that had been landing in the city for the last few days. The silly man didn't know how to tell the difference between griffins. It was almost funny, but she couldn't laugh yet.

When he reached for her, Cook was there with her biggest knife in hand. There would be a large cut of meat on the butcher table to justify the utensil/weapon.

"What's all the yelling out here?" Cook asked.

"Are you the barkeep?" There was surprise in the captain's thoughts and voice.

"Do I look like a barkeep? I'm the cook, you lunk. And what are you doing scaring my daughter?"

The man pulled back a bit, not willing to go up against a mother bear. "I'm here about a griffin that was seen landing in your yard."

"Right." Cook pulled Allay behind her to get in the guard's face. "You think that a griffin just landed in my yard again. You do know guards have been coming here every day for the past four days and you haven't found a single feather in our yard. Now would you quit scaring my customers?"

Allay left Cook to intimidate the guards and went to check the yard for griffin feathers. She found Missy already out there with three feathers in her hand.

"Here, get rid of these."

Kayla?

"Your friend is safe." Missy thought of the false wall at the back of the pantry where they usually hid their wheat stores during winter when the merchants couldn't get through the snows.

Can she stay with us?

"Of course." Missy smiled.

Allay took the feathers and headed for the little stable.

"It's nice to finally hear your voice."

Allay didn't touch the ground all the way to the stable and her own little hole where she kept her treasures. She added the feathers to the little glass beads and bits of metal she got from other travelers. They fit nicely beside the feathers she'd already collected from her friends.

CHAPTER SEVENTEEN
Kayla

Kayla smiled from the doorway as Missy bustled about the little room she insisted Kayla should stay in. "It's the least we can do for bringing Allay back safe and better," she'd said.

Allay warned her away from asking for a little closet or a place in the stable; it would be insulting. So here she was staring at the bed, now covered with fresh sheets, wondering how she could make that feel like the family sleeping circle or at least like snuggling up to a griffin.

The ways of the griffins were so similar to her family. Family groups hunt and play together. They sleep in circles so everyone's head is rested on someone else's body. Heat and dreams are shared in the night. She'd grown used to sleeping alone in the years of her walkabout. Jarron had laughed when she told him she missed the sleeping circles of home, but he took her to see how the street children sleep. They too slept in a pile. It was considered a sign of weakness to need that kind of sleep among the well-to-do of the city. She didn't care what the up-livers thought of her way of life. She still didn't.

Allay did care and that made the difference. So Kayla would isolate herself again, though the sense of family they developed sleeping in the griffin way in Crystal's cave made her dream of home.

"There you go." Missy stood in the middle of the room with her hands on her hips. "I hope it'll be comfortable enough for you. Let me know if you need anything else."

"Thank you." Kayla smiled and stepped into the room.

Other than the wooden walls, it was rather cave-like. Dark and small. It was on the highest floor, so the slope of the roof showed in the ceiling. There was one window tucked in an alcove and covered with dirty glass to let in sunlight. Otherwise, it was lit only by one small oil lamp set on the shelf next to the bed. The bed took most of the room. Directly across from it was a small fireplace with a fire set but not lit. Near the alcove was a small table with a chair.

"Dinner will be ready in about an hour."

"Thank you, but I won't be eating." Kayla considered the pillows and blankets on the bed. She could arrange them more like a nest.

"Oh, I'm sorry." Missy had moved toward the door, her smile gone.

"No offense to your cooking. It's just, well…"

She can't eat our food. Allay stood in the hall just beyond.

Missy jumped.

"She's right. I'll have to find my own food."

"Well, what do you eat?" Missy asked.

Kayla sighed. "So far, all I've found appetizing she tells me are poisons." Kayla waved to Allay. "Hedgelock is quite delicious."

"Oh." Missy tugged at her skirt. "Well…"

"Don't worry about it." Kayla smiled again. "I'm still figuring it out."

That settled it, for the moment. Missy smiled again, hugged Allay, then went back to running her inn. Allay stayed just long enough to assure Kayla that everything would be fine, but please don't let the other guests see her. Then she was off to do her part. So Kayla set about making the room as comfortable as she could. There wasn't much she could do. No amount of time living in little boxes had made them feel like home back in Kralt, and they weren't any better here.

She pushed the blankets and pillows around until she had a nice nest in the middle of the bed. All the while she worried over what Crystal had told her about the spell wrapped around her. The one demon who had appeared to be the leader when she woke up here held the key to sending her home. The spell had pulled her here because she fit the requirements he had for some task.

As far as she was concerned, if his own people couldn't do it, then it shouldn't be done. Power bent the people to the tasks they were meant for. It shaped them for the environment they were meant to live in. Fish had no legs and rabbits no fins. While each could survive a visit to the other's world, they could not live there. The only question, then, is she the fish or the rabbit? How long could she continue in this world to which she was not shaped?

No! Allay's mind jostled her out of her thoughts. *No!*

Kayla was halfway down the stairs before she remembered the caution not to be seen. She slowed just enough to seek camouflage before reaching the base of the stairs. She found it in the little room that separated the stairs from the common room. A hooded cloak that would cover everything from head to toe. As long as she didn't move too fast, no one would see her.

The panic from Allay's mind still flooded her thoughts, but Kayla forced herself to be cautious. Rushing never catches the rabbit, though the rabbit who rushes will get caught.

The main room was filled with men, if you could call them that. The smell was somewhat nauseating. These were the kinds of demons used to working for their living and they wore the dirt of their professions proudly. Most were seated around the large tables with ale mugs and stew bowls in front of them. But they were all turned toward the center of the room where one particularly large demon stood over Allay. The facial expressions of demons were difficult to read, but that body posture was clear enough. Predators had a way about them that never lied.

The demons seemed frozen by the shock of Allay's voice. That worked to Kayla's advantage. She had enough power to drop Allay through a portal to safety, but the predator was on her too close. Besides, that would draw too much attention. Kayla pushed her way through the crowd, keeping the cloak pulled tight.

"Release her." Kayla let a low growl fill her voice. At home, it would have been recognized she was laying claim to Allay.

The large demon huffed and pulled Allay closer. Now the panicky images coming from Allay were all to clear about the demon's intentions. They were worse than the smell he gave off.

"Release her or die." Kayla lowered the growl a step further.

"Says who?"

Kayla responded with a quick swipe of her claws across his upper thigh. He screamed with shock and pain but didn't release Allay. Another swipe at the arm holding the girl got the desired effect, but by then, it was too late. A fight had started and the demons were too thrilled to give it up.

Stupid demons. They didn't fight as a team. In fact, most of them were happy just pounding on each other. The chaos left no openings for Kayla to escape with Allay.

Allay, still in a bit of a panic, retreated from Kayla as well. She was going to get hurt in the middle of all the flying fists and chairs. Kayla took the second to focus and opened a small portal under Allay into the kitchen. That second left her open to a punch in her back.

She'd never been in a fight like this, but she had survived numerous stampedes. The principles were similar. Pay attention to everything and spend more effort on dodging than hitting. It took three more bruises before she learned to see the punches coming. She almost made it to the kitchen door before discovering demons can kick too. She stumbled into the kitchen only to face one of Cook's butcher knives.

"Keep your grubby hands off my daughter." Cook slashed with the knife, driving Kayla back against the wall.

"Sorry." Kayla lifted the hood. "Sorry."

"What in all the bloody stars do you think you are doing?" The knife was down, but Cook's face was just as menacing.

"I only meant to help." Kayla lifted her empty hands in surrender.

The brawl continued in the common room while Cook stared Kayla into submission. "This isn't help."

"What can I do?"

"Stop that fight before they break everything."

Kayla nodded, though she didn't know how to stop a fight.

Water. Allay imagined throwing glasses of water in all their faces.

That wouldn't work, but perhaps something similar. "I'll help clean up. I promise." She told cook just before she opened a complex portal in the middle of the lake with many smaller endpoints near the ceiling of the common room. The rain had an immediate effect on the demons, though they weren't any quieter. They forgot about punching each other and ran for the door.

Kayla closed the portal before the room became too flooded.

Cook stood slack-faced in front of Kayla. Missy appeared in the door to the common room, dripping from head to toe.

"What. Just. Happened?" Missy's posture reminded Kayla of the stiff-tailed stance Mother would take when one of the kits had done something particularly stupid.

A soft clatter drew all their attentions to the back door, just in time to see a small boy run off.

CHAPTER EIGHTEEN
Kayla

Kayla learned a lot about cleaning and repairing things in this world in the days that followed the fight. The demons also learned a thing or two, or so it seemed. Those who returned the next day were much more cautious about how they treated the women of the inn.

City guardsmen came about the rumors of a witch staying at the inn. Kayla kept herself hidden from them. Allay, however, stripped their thoughts for images of what they thought they were looking for. Kayla scolded her for being rude but joined in the laughter over the completely distorted images they had of who they were looking for.

You'll be able to hide easier now, Allay explained, since everyone looking for her would be seeking a bent old woman with a long pointed nose and fingernails longer than her fingers. *Keep yourself covered and they won't give you a second glance.*

She was right. Kayla ventured out into the city, covered by the cloak Cook decided she didn't need anymore and gloves Missy found in an old trunk. The women weren't convinced of the wisdom of Kayla seeking out the lord that had summoned her, but they couldn't offer any alternatives. Kayla needed a name at least. She'd tried drawing the symbols she could remember from her first awakening, but they said those were totems of a god.

Kayla wandered the streets, hoping to recognize the armor. All the fighting demons had worn the same armor. If she could find another with that armor and follow him to his nest, she could learn more about the one who had summoned her. A name at least would give her friends a way to help. Though Missy and Cook had already done more than could be expected for her. She was in debt past her tail with Allay as well. Debts she would never be able to repay.

Today, there was excitement in the streets and everyone moving in the same direction. Kayla had to move with them or risk being noticeable. She let the crowd push her along toward the castle at the top of the hill in the middle of the city. The chatter in the crowd didn't make a lot of sense to Kayla. They were talking about the king and the heir, but beyond that, she couldn't make out what they were all excited about. There was some controversy, clearly because people were staking out their sides and clumping into groups based on opinion.

When the crowd grew too tight, Kayla ducked into an alley. There she found the street kids, all just as excited as the people on the main street.

"The witch." One little girl wrapped in cloth that may have once been a dress pointed at Kayla. Her voice was soft and her eyes wide. It was impossible to tell anything of her true color under all the dirt.

The rest of the children turned to look at her. They fell silent, but their eyes were full of wonder.

"Do you grant wishes?" a small boy asked.

"Shh." A taller one cautioned.

"I'm not a witch." Kayla took a step forward slowly.

Street children knew more about the world than adults ever gave them credit for. In Kralt, the street children knew anyone could learn to wield the power, though conventional wisdom said only the special could be trained. The children were right, but the Magisters didn't want that known. It would lessen their power.

"You're green," the little boy said as though that would settle it.

"And you're pink. How odd."

They giggled. It didn't take much, as long as you were honest, to win the hearts of street kids.

"You're the odd one."

"Not where I come from."

More giggles. "You're here."

She smiled. "So I am. And I'm very curious. What's all the excitement about?"

"King Thorwin is going to announce the new heir."

"And it's a girl."

"They're going to let us see."

"If we can get close enough."

"I want to be a witch."

So many of them talking at once was hard to follow. One child,

82

somewhere in the mix, had a strong mind with a vivid imagination and just enough skill with mind speech for Kayla to catch the meaning.

"And you don't know how to get to the roofs?" she asked.

"Of course we do." The first small boy looked offended. "Just climb up there." He pointed to a corner in the buildings where the walls were close enough together to make climbing easy.

"Show me?"

All except the tallest boy, the one who was on the verge of becoming a man, ran to the corner and climbed to the top.

"What do you want?" the tall boy asked.

"I wanted a way to the roofs." Kayla admitted.

He didn't look impressed.

"After that, I'd like to go home."

He shifted to stand between her and the corner.

"I won't tell." She promised.

The other children called for the boy to follow them. He glared at her for a moment more before following them to the rooftops and disappearing over the ridges.

Kayla gave them a few moments to disperse before following them up to the roof. It was like a whole new city up here, with roads and buildings all around. The difference was here she could see into the distance where a large crowd had gathered in an open square near the castle. It wouldn't take long to get there on these rooftops, so long as she was careful.

Near the square, the roofs too were somewhat crowded. The children were nowhere to be seen, but there were others, mostly in cloaks and other concealing garments crouched in the shadows of every chimney. Kayla found a place to one side of a chimney while another man hid on the other side. He grumbled as she took her place.

In the square below, there was a stage with three very fancy chairs of different sizes. The largest in the middle and the two smaller to either side. Around the stage were several dozen soldiers in shining armor with impressive-looking spears standing shoulder to shoulder and keeping the crowd from approaching the stage. Opposite Kayla, there were rows of chairs on platforms just slightly above street level filled with demons in gaudy clothes. The chairs were also guarded by soldiers in the same fancy armor, though she could see more soldiers in different armor behind the chairs. She couldn't see any detail on those soldiers.

She considered trying to get to that side of the square to get a better look. She couldn't see a path directly there, and something was happening below.

Four horses were tied to a carriage. They looked like a blend of all the runners in the steppe, without antlers or horns. On top of the carriage, a demon held their leashes and guided them through the crowd. Below there were covered windows decorated with more bangles than all the demons in the chairs combined. More soldiers walked beside the carriage.

Her companion shifted on the other side of the chimney. The crowd below hushed. Even the fancy demons in their chairs stopped talking to each other except behind raised hands. Their attention was on the carriage. Kayla let it draw her attention too.

The carriage stopped directly behind the stage. From the ground, it would be hard to see what was happening, but Kayla's vantage gave her a perfect view. The door opened and three demons emerged. Their clothes were striking in the lack of gaudy bangles. Even from here, Kayla could see they were of a higher order. There were two adults and one girl about Allay's size. The king and queen and their daughter, of course.

Kayla marveled at how like the Magisters and up-dwellers of Kralt these fancy demons were. It was all about vision and ceremony. If she had to guess, those fancy-dressed demons were plotting how to improve their standing in the government. Those plots would be all about finding and revealing each other's secrets or embarrassing one or another. Most of what they did would have no impact at all on the people crowded around just for the chance to see them.

The demon on the other side of the chimney shifted some more. In fact, he was moving around enough to catch the attention of the guards around the stage. One was looking up this way. Kayla froze, knowing most wouldn't see anything at this range unless it moved. Her companion was drawing attention. She risked being seen herself to lean forward just enough to see his hands.

He was linking three long tubes into one. Used for blow darts, it would take a lot of breath but give the darts accuracy over distance. They weren't the kind of tubes that would work well with lenses, though that would make more sense if you were watching an event from afar.

The king, queen and princess were just making their way onto the stage. The crowd cheered, making it hard to hear anything of the king's speech. Closer to hand, she could hear the demon muttering to himself.

"Come on, line up pretty now."

The royals did just as he said, standing in a row right in front of their chairs. The first dart flew with a heavy puff that didn't come from

84

his lungs. The second flew barely a breath after. When the third puff came, Kayla opened three portals. Dropping the royals into the only place she could think of. Her little room at the Broken Ale. A fourth portal landed the assassin and his dart gun in the king's chair. A fifth dropped her on her bed.

A moment later, she realized that wasn't the best plan. The princess screamed for her guards while she struggled to stand. The king was already dead and the queen gasped for breath and held her neck.

Kayla rushed to help, knocking the princess back. She pulled the dart from the queen's neck and tried to suck the poison out. The princess caught Kayla in the gut with a well-placed kick. From some-where, she managed to find a pair of daggers to threaten Kayla with.

"Leave her alone." The princess used the same low tones Kayla had when she'd warned the demon off Allay.

"There is poison," Kayla said, but it was too late. The queen gasped one last breath and lay still.

That was when Missy, Cook, and Allay burst through the door. There was a moment when no one moved, spoke, or even breathed. Then they all started in at once.

"Guards! Guards!"

"What in the name of Odran?"

"I was trying to—"

"Mercy and light!"

Did you kill them?

Missy stepped up with her hands raised. "Enough. One at a time."

"I demand to be released. Where are my guards?" The princess brandished her daggers at Missy.

"Your Majesty, your guards aren't here. And if we simply let you walk out of here, you will be dead or a slave before you get halfway back to the palace." Missy took the mothering tone that usually worked with the drunk demons who wanted to do something stupid.

"Are you threatening me?"

"No." Missy turned to Kayla. "What happened?"

Kayla explained about finding her way to the roof and sitting next to the assassin. She talked over the princess' complaints that she should have stopped the man rather than kidnapped the entire royal family.

"The darts were poisoned. I didn't kill them." Kayla finished, staring at the princess.

"I believe you." Missy assured her. "But what are we going to do with them?"

You have to send them back. Allay climbed up on the bed beside Kayla. *If they're found here, we'll all be executed.*

The princess flattened herself against the wall, eyes wide, staring at Allay.

"Don't be silly." Kayla projected to the girl. "She has no other way to talk."

"Quit it." Missy smacked Allay and Kayla on the back of the head.

Kayla fought her instinct to attack back, though her claws did appear in her hands for a long enough moment to scare the princess more. This was the kind of rescue that would make for good stories around the evening fire when she had grandchildren to entertain. For now, though, she could only focus on how poorly she was doing.

"Your Highness." Missy bowed to the girl. "Please take a moment to calm yourself and think on this situation."

"How do you expect me to relax when you've sent a demon to kill me?" The princess pointed at Kayla without moving her eyes from Missy's.

"Believe me, Highness." Missy pulled herself up straight. "If Kayla had intended to kill you, you would be dead. I have no control over her other than that of a friend."

"You admit to being friends with demons?" This time she glanced at Kayla.

"I am no demon." Kayla bowed the way Missy had. "I was torn from my world by a male of your kind to perform a task."

"What task?"

"He wasn't smart enough to learn my language before calling me. If he said it, I didn't understand." Kayla held the girl's eyes, willing her to believe.

The princess pulled herself up about a quarter inch taller. She said nothing, but with a slight nod, she accepted what they had told her. A step forward told Missy she would stay but needed a better room than this one.

Kayla watched the girl, who gave all the indications of being a quivering mass of emotions, walk quietly with strength out of the room after Missy.

CHAPTER NINETEEN
Allay

There were more guards than ever in the streets of the city. Allay smiled and bobbed her head each time she passed one, or more commonly, a group of them. They didn't pay her much attention. Why would they care about the little peasant girl who never said anything, when they were searching for the rogue mage who had stolen the royal family?

And odd choice of word: "stolen." That's the word she heard over and over on their voices and in their heads. As if the king, queen, and princess were precious works of art rather than people. If that was really the way that people thought of them, it must be awful to be royal. It was no wonder Silvanie acted so odd when Missy and Cook tried to make her feel at home. It made sense, then, that she didn't think of love when they planned for how to return her to the palace safely. She thought only of duty. She thought about all the things that she would have to do to make the transition of power stick. That was going to be all the harder because her father hadn't made her the official heir yet.

All the more reason not to wish to be a princess.

Allay clutched the letter Silvanie had written to the one person in the palace she felt she could trust. It had his name on it and Silvanie's seal pressed into the wax that held it closed. Between the two, it should keep Allay from being run off by the gate guards. If that worked, she only had to hope Sir Delare would read and follow the princess' instructions. Other than Sir Delare, Allay was to keep her mind to herself.

It took all of Allay's self-control to keep her hands from shaking as she approached the palace gate. There were more guards than usual here too. There were the two with the great lances who were always there. Their lances were crossed even before Allay stepped close to the gate. With them were four more guards in full armor, long swords tipped to the ground in front of them. Despite the relaxed pose they held, Allay could feel the intense sense of danger they felt. Anyone, and everyone, could be a threat and they didn't know where that threat would come from.

Allay tried to shrink even farther into her dress. This plan didn't feel so safe anymore. She would follow it through, of course, but now being the mute little peasant girl wasn't the shield it was supposed to be. The guards weren't supposed to be the ones who were scared. They had the weapons. They had the training. They were also the ones who would deliver her message to Sir Delare and open the door for Silvanie to return home.

"Halt."

Allay didn't see which of the guards had spoken. She stopped where she was and held out the note.

"State your purpose." The guard just to the right of the two with crossed spears spoke.

Allay waved the note slightly. She prayed that he would figure it out but imagined them throwing her in the dungeon because she couldn't answer their question.

"Girl, I'm speaking to you." The guard lifted his sword, bringing the tip up to point directly at her.

The guard to his left leaned in to say something Allay couldn't hear.

"Step forward, slowly," the guard commanded.

People had stopped to watch what was happening. All around the little square, business had come to a halt. Allay wanted nothing more than to run from all the attention and hide. Did they have to stare so openly? Allay locked her eyes on the guard whose sword still pointed at her and walked forward. It felt like she was walking right onto his sword even though the tip was still feet away.

"What have you got there?" he asked when she was one step from being able to touch the tip of his sword with an outstretched hand.

Allay held up the letter again. It was like a pantomime. She decided that running away to join a players company wasn't any better than being a princess.

A man came from behind her to snag the letter out of her hand.

"A child with a letter addressed to me." Sir Delare knocked the tip of the guard's sword down and away from Allay. "When were you going to tell me about this?"

"Sir, we didn't know what it was."

Sir Delare snorted. "You'd best come with me or they'll be claiming they didn't know what you were either by the end of the day." He offered an open hand to Allay. *It's all right. I won't hurt you.*

Allay swallowed her shock long enough to take his hand. She'd never heard another human's voice in her head like that. Crystal had said it was rare. Allay thought she meant she was the only one.

"So how did you come by a letter written in Silvanie's hand with Silvanie's crest to seal it?"

Allay only looked at him, tightening the control over her own mind. She wasn't supposed to reveal her ability until after he'd read the letter. So far, he'd turned it every which way, but the seal remained unbroken.

He brought her to a small pub just off the central square and announced to the barkeep he was going to use the private room in back. The room was much like the private dining room at the Broken Ale—just big enough for a table and four chairs with a painted window and candle sconces all the way around. Sir Delare left the letter on the table while he lit the candles himself. All the while, she could feel him poking at the edges of her mind exactly the way Kayla told her not to do.

"Well, you are just full of surprises." He sat in one of the chairs and waved for her to sit in the other. "I'm guessing you won't tell me a darned thing until I read that letter. And the most interesting part is I have to guess."

Allay wondered if Silvanie knew this man was also a mind-speaker. She hesitated to sit, though this wasn't the Broken Ale and she wasn't a worker here. The chairs and table showed no signs of the regular bar fights that marked all of the Ale's furniture.

The barkeep entered with a tray that he set on the middle of the table and left without saying a word. He'd brought two mugs of some fruity drink and a small plate of cut fruit.

Sir Delare laughed. "Well, if that doesn't prove it. Darren is the most astute of barkeeps I've ever met. Nothing but fruit to signal our privacy."

Allay didn't see the joke. She just wanted him to open the letter so she could finish this job and go back to being boring little Allay. Had she ever wished to be part of a bard's tale? If so, she took it back.

He set one of the mugs in front of her and took the other for himself. Then he finally picked up the letter and cracked the seal. The small smile he had worn since he first took the letter from her hands dropped away and let his face show the lines of age. His mind also lost the tight control he'd had over it, letting her feel some of the strain he felt over this situation.

"So you are supposed to show me the situation." He looked directly into her eyes. Just the way Silvanie had told her he would when he accepted the letter.

Allay opened her memory of Silvanie and her parents arriving in the Broken Ale. She remembered Missy and Cook laying out and caring for the bodies of the king and queen. There were the discussions over dinner about how to return the princess and the bodies to the palace without drawing too much attention or putting the princess in more danger.

"Until she is behind the palace walls again, the best protection we can offer her is to keep her hidden." Kayla's words from her place at the table.

Kayla insisted she be included in the message. Allay, Missy, and Cook objected, but Silvanie agreed.

"Tell me, show me, how you became so skilled in manipulating your mind." Sir Delare held Allay's eyes in a way that prevented her from turning away.

Kayla had warned her of this possibility. *Curiosity is a constant. Respond with strength.*

Allay pushed the pain of growing up without a voice into his head. She let him see how the griffins were more like her than the people of her city. She also let him see the training she'd received from Crystal and Kayla.

The old dragon trusts the demon? Then I shall trust her as well. He pushed her thoughts back to her.

This time it was Allay's turn to feel the pain of growing up different. Since he could talk, he told people what he heard in his head and was chased from his home for it. They called him demon touched wherever he went until he found his way to Crystal's mountain.

"Well then, it seems you are more than others see. It would be a shame to let you go."

You can't keep me here.

"I meant to offer you a job." His smile was back in place. So was the wall around his mind. "Someone with your skills will make it much more difficult for the princess's enemies to interfere."

Allay shook her head. She wanted to get back to the Broken Ale and her life with Missy and Cook and… No, she could live without the drunks and their grabby hands.

"Can I convince you to help until the coronation?" He let her see the kinds of problems Silvanie would face at court just to get to the coronation. "It's not the assassins I fear so much as the lords themselves."

He was as skilled as Kayla at manipulating his thoughts, but somehow it felt very different. Allay wasn't so sure she wanted to trust him.

I'm just a peasant.

"A girl, a child, and a peasant." He spoke as though all of those were assets. "Besides, you are needed inside the palace to return her majesty."

Allay scowled. He was right. Kayla needed her in the palace to open the portal.

"Well then, drink up. We wouldn't want to insult Darren, and he makes some wonderful juice. Besides, we are going to have to wait for the changing of the guard to get you through that gate without more spectacle." He lifted his own mug.

CHAPTER TWENTY
Lord Corawin Tromadin

Corawin strode into the council room as though he owned it. By the end of the day, he would. The whole system was in a terrible state of chaos since the disappearance of the entire royal family. Every lord on the council would be looking for an angle on this, and he intended to be the first back on his feet. Only the one who planned this would be faster, but then he'd have a guilty conscience to trip him up.

A quick look around the room made it clear that there were two camps among the lords. Those who believed the royals would return in their usual gaudy colors and jewels, and those who believed they were dead in the somber colors and jewels of mourning. Corawin stood with the second camp. Other than the rings of his family and station, he'd left all the jewelry at home today. He hadn't dressed in this much black since his father's funeral. That too had been for show. He'd been grateful the old man had died before he had to have him killed to take power.

"Lord Tromadin." Callay did his best to blend into both camps. He was layered in dark colors with more than his usual array of pendants, necklaces, and rings to fill in the color. "I'm pleased to see you today."

"Why wouldn't I be here?" Corawin moved farther into the room, edging his way toward the head of the table.

"Last reports of you were hunting in Farthingay's northern hills." Callay snagged a goblet of wine from a passing servant. "I'll tell you, Lord Farthingay is less than pleased to hear of your exploits. He's been ranting on and on about disturbing the dragon and something or other about needing to keep the peasants calm."

"He'll be happy to know I wasn't hunting his precious dragon." Corawin huffed. "If he's so concerned about the peasants, why doesn't he do something about the dragon?"

Callay snorted at the old joke. "Seriously, though, you've made some enemies with that hero of yours."

"Shut your mouth." Corawin kept his voice even. "She's as much yours as mine. At least I've been trying to clean up our mess."

"Yes, you've made it perfectly clear to all that you are taking responsibility." Callay smiled and walked away.

Corawin took a moment to curse his fellow lord to all the gods he could think of.

"Lord Corawin Tromadin, you old scoundrel." Lord Haring thumped him on the shoulder. "Heard you were having some sort of woman trouble. Ha-ha-ha. Hope you got over that. Ha-ha."

"Yeah, I solved that little issue." Corawin forced a grin at the graying lord. His son should take a more active role in moving this man on. "I hope you don't mind."

Haring looked blank for a moment before deciding it was a joke and laughing. Corawin slipped between a couple lords speaking in hushed tones, only to run into Lord Farthingay.

"Just the man I was hoping to see." Farthingay was one of the more colorful members of the court, even when dressed for mourning as he was now.

"So I've heard." Corawin tried to turn away.

Farthingay followed him. "I hope you didn't disturb the dragon on your wild chase through my lands."

"Of course not."

The herald thumped his staff three times. "Her Royal Majesty, Princess Silvanie."

Corawin jumped. When had she returned? How did she escape the demon? He knew his demon had taken them. Who else could have made those distinctive holes in the stage? He went through the motions of bowing to the reigning monarch along with the other lords.

The princess entered in full mourning, complete with a black veil. From what little he could see of her, she didn't have any marks of her encounter with the demon. She walked without a limp and didn't favor one side or the other. That couldn't be right. Everyone had seen her fall through the blue hole.

By the time Corawin recovered his wits, she was standing at the head of the table with a girl dressed as a maid to one side and Sir Delare to the other.

94

"Attention," the princess called.

The lords quickly found their places around the great table. Corawin hadn't made it as close as he would have liked to the head, but he was still close enough to take some control when she lost it.

"I would like to announce the deaths of His Royal Majesty King Thorwin and Her Royal Majesty Queen Theara. They were assassinated by a man from the Tragale Tribe of the Eastern Mountains. Naturally, there will be a full investigation into who hired this man and their purpose."

"If you have the assassin, why not just ask him?" Lord Farthingay asked.

Silvanie nodded in acknowledgment of the question. "Because he killed himself before questioning could begin."

Sir Delare gave a slight gesture. It appeared to be aimed at Corawin, but he didn't know what it meant.

"As the king is dead, Sir Delare has been relieved of his duties as king's own. However, I have asked him to stay on to help with the investigation. His skills that served him well as king's own will help keep the investigation quick."

Corawin seethed under that assumption. "If he was such a great king's own, the king wouldn't be dead."

There were murmurs of assent all along the table.

"Lord Tromadin, you know better than most that my duty was never as body guard." Sir Delare bowed with a grin just barely visible on his lips. "King Thorwin was my friend as well as my leader. I am honored by Her Majesty's request."

"I expect all of you, as lords of the council, to cooperate fully in the investigation," Silvanie said. "Funeral arrangements are being finalized and will be announced within a day. I expect the council will be in attendance, so please adjust your travel plans accordingly."

What travel plans could she be referring to? Such presumption.

"We need to discuss the succession." Corawin stood. "Since the death of Prince Travis, we have not had an heir apparent. Such neglect has made this tragedy even more of a problem than it needed to be."

"Your lordship." Silvanie looked directly at him. "According to our laws, the succession is clear. The closest living relative shall take the throne upon the death of the previous monarch."

She was sweet in her tone and poison with her words.

"That is not how the law reads."

The maid handed Silvanie a small scroll. Silvanie passed it to the lord to her right. "I think you should spend more time among the records."

Each lord opened the scroll, read it, and passed it on. Corawin couldn't see anything in their expressions to warn him what was in that scroll. When he opened it, he found a copy of the succession law, exactly as she had quoted it, signed by the head clerk of the records office.

Corawin set his jaw and passed the scroll to the next. He couldn't let that paper force them to accept a woman on the throne. "Nevertheless, you are both too young and too inexperienced to lead this country through this crisis."

More murmuring of assent from his fellow lords. He had more support than he'd anticipated.

"You mean I'm too *woman* for the job."

All the murmurs were silenced by that.

"We need a strong leader."

"I agree, but if you wish to make a claim against my taking the throne, then you should all know, the closest male relative is my uncle, Lord Charwin."

Lord Charwin started from his seat at the far end of the table. He was King Thorwin's half brother and twenty years older than the old king. He was a member of the council only because he was so closely related to the king. He spent more time in the council room asleep than drinking, and more time drinking than paying attention to the discussion at hand.

The maid offered a second scroll. Corawin didn't need to see it to know it would contain the lineage that would prove Charwin was second in line for the throne. He didn't doubt it would show the entire council and their place in the line. What did surprise him when the scroll came to his hand was his own wife was three places above him on the lineage chart.

"Now that is settled. We will need to begin preparations for my coronation."

CHAPTER TWENTY-ONE
Kayla

Like a caged animal, Kayla paced the length of the little room Silvanie had set aside for her. The room was beautiful with tall windows that captured the sunlight and made candles unnecessary. The walls were covered with gold and silver patterns inlaid into the marble. Where the walls weren't decorated directly, there were tapestries showing all manner of scenes. The one across from the door showed a griffin defending the palace against invaders. Such a difference from how the griffins were treated now.

This thought barely distracted her from the council meeting one floor below her. She could see and hear it all when she linked with Allay. What she saw were the two fancy-dressed demons who were there the day they called her from Kralt. The day they took her away from Jarron and everything she knew and loved. They were the reason her street children wouldn't get the help they needed, and they were sitting there in the council meeting acting as though they had nothing to feel guilty about.

When the one called Tromadin spoke, he was anything but respectful. Kayla couldn't understand why Silvanie would allow him to speak like that without slashing his ears. She'd had to sever the link to Allay before her anger bled through to the girl.

Allay was doing wonderfully in her role as Silvanie's maid. No one wondered that she never spoke a word because maids weren't supposed to in a meeting like that. What they didn't know was she was feeding Silvanie all the thoughts and attitudes she could pick up. Her skill with her mind speech was becoming more flexible and more powerful with practice. It was clear the girl's power was more than just mind speech. She would learn tricks Kayla could barely dream of.

The meeting is over. Allay broke into Kayla's thoughts.

Can I come kill them now? Kayla was only half joking. There were no kidnappers among the Felani tribes. Not because there were no incentives for doing such things, but because the penalty for doing so was death by the claws of whoever caught you. The stories told that most kidnappers died at the hands of the victims. She'd seen that law in action when she was still too small to do more than play. Members of a rival tribe came to demand that she be sent back to the southern forests where she belonged. They could easily have taken her there themselves, but without the consent of Mother, they would forfeit their lives to do so.

These demons were no better. They used their magic... No, they used the magic of others to force her against her will to this place. By all rights, they should be dead.

Don't kill them directly. Allay relayed Silvanie's words. *They need to be scandalized first. Then you will have the right to kill them, though that may not be the best punishment.*

Kayla slashed at an imaginary lord. *How am I supposed to scandalize them?*

Wait, we'll be there soon. Allay's mind felt tired.

It was too much to ask of the girl to use her skills so heavily in one day. She was still just a kit and new to the idea that her ability to hear thoughts was more than just a curse. Kayla should remember a kit needed time to work up strength before she could be sent on a real hunt.

"Sure, I agree that Tromadin is a troll and needs to be taken down a peg, but he'll expect something," Sir Delare was saying as they entered the little room where Kayla had spent the last half hour pacing. "Did you even try the chairs?"

"I'm not much for sitting around," Kayla said. There was something about this man that made her keep her guard up.

"Of course not. You are a hunter." He bared his extraordinarily white teeth at her in what some might call a smile. She saw no humor in it.

"Were you able to identify the lords who called you?" Silvanie stepped in front of Delare.

"I heard the name of Lord Tromadin, but the other was present but never named." Kayla pushed an image of the second fancy demon to Allay, who relayed the image to Silvanie.

"Do you know him?"

"Of course." She drew her lips in tight, as though keeping something from escaping her mouth. "That's Lord Callay. A toady of a man, always looking for an angle to be in someone else's plan for his own gain."

"Callay?" Delare laughed. "I should have guessed."

Kayla fixed him with a stare meant to pin a wayward kit to the ground.

"Callay is, as Her Majesty says, always looking for a way to be part of someone else's plan." Delare blanked his face. "I doubt he's ever had an original thought in his life. I have heard he is a cruel master."

"Then why don't his people leave?" Kayla asked. These demons made about as much sense as the city dwellers she was born to. They spent more time worrying about the structures of their lives than actually living them. A poor leader among the tribes lost her followers to other tribes.

They aren't allowed to. Allay filled Kayla's mind with the rules of living in a lord's county. Even the rules didn't make sense.

"There was a woman I heard of once who did just that." Delare moved behind one of the high-backed chairs as though seeking protection from some threat. "I don't know what became of her. She was said to be a cook in Callay's house until something drove her to leave. Find her and she might be willing to tell you what was so bad to drive a woman from such good employment."

"A cook? Someone who cooks for others?" Kayla asked.

"That's what I heard." Delare had a tight grip on the back of the chair. "I never was able to find her."

"Why would you be looking for her?" Silvanie asked.

"It was my duty to investigate all the lords. Whenever there was a rumor of misdeeds, your father wanted to know as much as I could learn about the real situation." Delare's knuckles were turning white.

He wasn't being completely honest and felt guilty about it. That much leaked through the curtain he'd drawn across his mind.

"Tell me this much." Kayla shifted to stand directly in front of him with only the chair between them. "Would this woman have found employment with another lord or with her lover?"

Delare looked away. The white of his knuckles spread to cover his whole fingers.

"I've met this woman you speak of," Kayla said.

Allay filled her mind with curiosity. Silvanie stared at her with eyes twice their usual size.

"Missy and Cook, the owners of the Broken Ale." Kayla let

Allay feel all her thoughts about the two women, especially the way neither of them used "Cook" as a name, but a title. There were the hints from Delare as well, like his disgust at the thought of two women having that kind of relationship.

Silvanie brought her expression under control. "You amaze me." She shook her head. "I would suggest you start there for your revenge, then."

"What about Tromadin?" Kayla asked. "If, as you say, Callay attaches himself to others' ideas, then it is Tromadin's fault I am here."

Silvanie looked away. "Because Tromadin is the kind of man who will have protected himself, but not his associates. You will make him suffer more through the scandal you bring down on Callay first." She lifted her eyes to meet Kayla's. "Also, Tromadin is most likely to know how to send you back. He won't as long as he thinks you might still do his bidding. Make him see you as a threat and you'll have leverage."

Kayla didn't like to play things at such angles. She much preferred direct action. She had learned about politics and indirect action from Jarron and saw how effective it could be when a frontal attack wasn't possible.

"Why should I care if he thinks of me as a threat?"

"Because if you aren't a threat, to him you are nothing." Silvanie held her head up even farther. "He has no patience for women, and you are clearly a woman of your people."

That made even less sense than the rules about people being unable to leave a bad leader just because of the conditions of your birth.

"Your ways baffle me." Kayla shook her head.

"They baffle me too." Silvanie smiled. It was a genuine smile filled with joy. "I'm going to miss you when you break this spell and return home."

Kayla nodded. There were things she would lose as well when this adventure came to an end. All the more reason to take out her frustrations on the demons who caused all of this.

Kayla opened a portal to the Broken Ale. *Are you coming?*

Allay shook her head. It wasn't hard to see the girl was taken with the kind of work she was doing now. As she should be, though there was conflict in her thoughts as well. Her moms were going to be disappointed. At least she wasn't traveling beyond the borders.

As she stepped through the portal, she moved from the quiet of a private room in the palace to the bustle of a tavern kitchen in the middle of the midday meal.

100

"Pull the bread out of the oven," Cook ordered when she saw Kayla standing there.

Kayla smiled. Just like one who is doing the job to which she was born. She took orders as best she could until the all the people had their meals and it was up to Missy to keep up with the drink orders.

"You've got something to say?" Cook asked, dropping into a chair in the little nook where the family ate breakfast.

"Allay is happy." Kayla started.

"And not coming home." Cook growled.

Kayla shook her head. "Not right away. She's found a place for herself that seems to have been made especially for her."

"Working for the royals. No better than the lords."

"She's working for Silvanie." Kayla perched on the chair opposite Cook.

Mother always said, "A lie can hold only so much stress, but the truth picks up what's left." Any mother would stress about a child heading out into the world. Mother fretted about the camp for days before and after Ari left for walkabout. Her fretting started even sooner when it was Kayla's turn. Father must have gone mad by the time Kayla reached the border to the jungle lands. Now it was proving true with Cook, showing her disdain for the leaders of her people.

"You weren't always a tavern cook, were you?" Kayla asked.

Cook looked up with surprise. "What makes you say that?"

"Delare stopped looking for you when he realized you were in love with Missy."

"Sir Delare?" Cook popped from the table. She wrung the towel that usually lived on her shoulder. "That pompous stuffed shirt of an idiot who got himself all puffed up when His Majesty named him king's own?" She snorted again, then went to scrub the already clean work counter in the middle of the kitchen. "Why would he even start looking for me?"

Kayla kept the table between them but reached across to stop Cook's hands from scrubbing her hands raw. "Because he believed you know something about Lord Callay."

"What's that to do with you?" she screeched. "Get out of my kitchen."

Missy was at Cook's side, holding her still. "What's this about, then? You'd better have a damned fine reason for bringing up that bastard."

Mother had a jaw with teeth designed for ripping flesh from bone. When she wanted to, she could make you think they were specifically meant for tearing the flesh from *your* bones. The look on Missy's face was scarier.

"That bastard is one of the demons who brought me here." Kayla forced her hands to release her claws.

The two women stood in stunned silence for a long heartbeat. Then, tears and shaking ended, Cook patted Missy on the shoulder and left. Missy watched her go even after she was out of sight.

"You'll get nothing from her about that man." Missy waved Kayla to the table. "Even I don't know what he did to her. I'll tell you this. If you can bring that evil son of a cat low, we'll be grateful."

"I need to know what he's done." Kayla thought about what Silvanie said about scandals and how it hurt lords more than watching each other get killed.

Missy nodded. "I don't know and she won't tell. But there may be one who will."

Kayla leaned in to be sure to catch all the details on how to find Marissa. A woman who still lived just outside of Callay's county village. When Missy was finished, Kayla patted her hand and promised to get Cook's revenge on the lord.

CHAPTER TWENTY-TWO
Tromadin

Corawin tried to keep his smile properly welcoming while somber enough for the occasion. Half the lords of the council had agreed to gather in his city estate after the official funeral for their monarchs. The funeral and required mourning period gave him some time to change the coronation. He needed more to bring any plan to seat himself on the throne to fruition. The demon just added a complication that would drain even more time.

Silvanie was a tricky one, skilled in the deceptions women required to get their way. Though half her power had to come from that loathsome peasant, Delare. How a man born in a barn could catch the attention of the king was inconceivable. That he would be able to take that opportunity and get himself named to the highest post in the land was disgusting. Now, of course, he was working his illegitimate magic to keep himself in power.

"It's a dilemma, no question," Lord Callay was saying when Corawin approached. "How can you convincingly argue that Silvanie is a worse leader than Charwin. The man just doesn't know how to pay attention."

"Oh, he can pay attention," Lord Sarin responded. "Have you seen him at dinner?"

They all laughed.

"A good point." Corawin stepped in. "But they aren't our only options."

"So you say." Sarin raised his wine glass at Corawin. "But the genealogy is clear. Charwin is the king's brother."

"Ah, but not by the queen mother," Corawin said. "One must ask if a peasant's son can be a legitimate king."

He let that little surprise sit for a moment.

"What are you suggesting?" Sarin asked.

"That the genealogy isn't the only provision in our laws." Corawin grinned inwardly that he'd managed to find the other way a king might be chosen. "A king can be named by the gods without regard to heredity."

"You want to leave it to gods?" Callay looked at him with skepticism. "I wouldn't think—"

"It's a gamble to be sure." Sarin cut him off. "The gods are unpredictable."

Corawin allowed his expression to fall just a bit. "I will admit it would make it hard to plan for a time, but considering our current options..."

"Oh." Sarin gasped. The conversation was well on its way, and Corawin didn't have to add anything more to their wild suppositions. The possibility that anyone could be named gave them all hope. Hope led to plans, which in turn made the possibility more appealing. A few more seeds planted and there would be enough call in the council to force that upstart girl to call for the panel of priests herself.

She had enough to worry her little head about with the loss of her parents to that demon. A girl really shouldn't take on too much in the time of mourning. Or at anytime really. He let himself be drawn into a conversation about the strange way the king and queen were killed.

"Strange indeed. I wonder how the princess managed to survive." He dropped his voice as though he didn't want to be overheard. "I heard they were poisoned. I wonder how she became immune."

Another conversation full of doubt and wild accusations. It wouldn't be long before that group of lords came to the conclusion that Silvanie herself was behind the attack. It would add more appeal to leaving the successions to the gods.

At the same time, it did open some questions of his own. No one had yet shown any signs that they were behind the assassinations. If he'd known it could be that simple, he might have gone to the mountain people himself. He would have expected the lord responsible to have made his move by now. None of the spies he paid too much for had any information to suggest that any of the lords were benefiting from the current situation. They were all scrambling to put plans in place to advance their positions.

He shook his head. He could worry over that nonsense later.

He had conversations to start and ideas to plant.

"Who would you put on the throne?"

The question made its way around a circle of minor players. They all had their allies and partners they thought could give them something for their support. Theoretical support. They were minor players for their lack of imagination. When they turned the question to him, he smiled.

"Myself, of course." Let them see how true ambition could work, and when they tried to follow his example, he'd cut them down. "And I already have two sons to ensure the succession doesn't become a problem for at least one more generation."

Laughter. Let them laugh. The idea would grow in that light.

"But I have two sons as well." Farthingay glared at Corawin across the small group.

"Have either of them killed their first fox yet?" Corawin remembered not to glare. Politics was a pain.

More laughter, as everyone knew Farthingay's twin sons were still struggling to stay atop a horse when they could get there. Not their fault. They were born small and stayed that way. At that age and size, it was a wonder Farthingay even allowed them to try.

"Seriously, though, gentlemen, we need to think of who would make the best leader in these chaotic times. "We can't just leave it to chance." Corawin smiled and raised his glass to get them all to do the same.

The proper application of alcohol to conspiracies could change the course of the country. He tried not to think of how much this would cost him or where that gold would come from. As long as the lords thought of him favorably while considering his theories, it would be worth every bit he could wring from his county.

"I'm not so sure."

Corawin missed who said that.

"That little girl maid she keeps by her side all the time, there's something wrong." Lord Sarin spoke again, now in hushed tones with Callay.

"What do you think is going on?" Callay glanced at Corawin but kept his attention on Sarin.

Corawin moved out of Sarin's vision but stayed close enough to hear what the lord had to say.

"I don't think she's a maid at all." Sarin looked around and leaned in closer to Callay. "I think she's some kind of mage sent to keep the princess in line." He stood up and nodded.

Well, this was an interesting theory, though he couldn't see the benefits yet. Anything that brought doubt on Silvanie could only be good.

"She's just a maid." Callay scoffed. "Like any other maid. Have we really seen enough of the princess before to know who her favorites are?"

"That's just it. We haven't, but my spies in the palace say she's new. They say Sir Delare brought her in just before the princess came back."

Delare again. That man was a pain in Corawin's side and would have to be dealt with. That was another headache for another time. This theory that the princess was being controlled could have some use. He fed it to several more lords as he continued to circulate among the crowds.

Nothing was decided by the end of the evening, but thoughts were flowing in the directions he wanted. When he became king, these kinds of politics would be outlawed.

"Well, a success I would think." Callay stood in the foyer as though he were a second host for the gathering.

Corawin smiled but said nothing. He was tired and wished for nothing more than his bed and an early morning to prepare for his next meeting with lords.

"The number of theories you planted into their minds was astonishing. How did you come up with all of that?"

"I didn't. They are perfectly capable of fooling themselves if you give them enough room to think." Corawin edged closer to the door.

Callay held his place.

"Did you need something?"

"Just wondering how you were coming in finding that demon you loosed on the country?"

"You were there too, and I have records to prove it if I have to." Corawin had spent enough time being nice tonight.

"The assassin, that was you?" Callay moved closer. "You don't have to say anything. I know enough to convince that idiot Delare it was you."

"And I know enough to prove to any court that you have betrayed your king and country as well. Are we done with the threats yet?" Corawin yawned.

Dealing with a man like Callay needed more attention than he had at the moment. Perhaps more than he'd used when setting off on this plan. A mistake he wouldn't make twice.

"That girl. You know where she came from."

Corawin snorted. "You can think that all you like, but she's just a serving girl. One who knows how to keep her mouth shut."

Callay shook his head. "It's more than that. I saw the way they interacted."

What a waste of time. Corawin could live without all this nonsense about the subtleties of serving girls. The girl was a servant, nothing more. She was one who knew to keep her mouth shut. That was a valuable skill and probably the reason she held such a favored position in the princess' court.

"They were talking. I'm not sure how, but they were definitely talking to each other." Callay stepped even closer to Corawin as though there might be someone listening. "Only the stars know what the girl was saying to the princess, but the princess was giving orders as well."

"You need to sleep it off." Corawin pointed to the door. "I don't have time to listen to you fall for the same tricks we just pulled on the rest of the council."

Callay pulled back, tightened his lips, and left. Good riddance. Corawin shook his head. He would have thought the man smart enough to recognize the effects of his own scheme.

CHAPTER TWENTY-THREE
Allay

Allay missed Kayla. Ever since Silvanie had sent her off to deal with Lord Callay, Allay hadn't heard anything from her. Even Sharl didn't know where she had gone, though the griffins watched for her.

It wasn't that Allay was lonely. Some of the other servants got over their fear of her ability within a few days. Enough of them that she had companions when she wasn't working with Princess Silvanie. When she was working with the princess, her mind was so taken up with the thoughts of others that she didn't have time to be lonely then either.

It was only in the quiet just before she fell asleep that she worried whether what she was doing was good or evil. She'd never thought about her ability as something that could change the world. She heard and saw what other people thought. Now she used their private thoughts to give Silvanie an advantage. She wanted to help the princess. In the dark at the end of the day, a small thought that maybe she was cheating lingered at the back of her mind.

Kayla would know. So would Crystal. Sir Delare should too, but he kept his thoughts so tightly concealed Allay couldn't tell what he really thought of anything. She got the impression he could read her as easily as she read the lords in the council chamber, but he never said or thought anything about it.

"Are you ready?" Silvanie asked as they approached the audience chamber.

Allay nodded. Today the game would be played one on one. One lord at a time would come to the audience chamber so Sir Delare could ask them questions. Allay was to show the princess any thoughts that were at odds with what was said, or left unsaid, in answer to Sir Delare's questions.

Sir Delare, of course, was doing the same thing for himself. No one knew exactly what Sir Delare did. He explained it as a skill at "reading people." Princess Silvanie didn't believe he would tell her everything. She didn't think about it much, but there was an argument between Sir Delare and King Thorwin that made the princess lose trust in her father's most trusted friend. Yet another issue that Kayla would be able to explain, except she wasn't here.

Wherever she was, Allay wished her well and a speedy return.

The audience chamber was a room at least as large as the council chamber, only there wasn't a table taking up the middle. At one end, there was a raised area with a throne so gilded and upholstered it would be a shame to sit on it. Along the walls were highly carved benches that looked like they might even be comfortable. In a corner near the raised area, almost hidden by the tapestries, sat a clerk at a writing desk. The clerk seemed barely aware of anything going on in the room; he was concerned only with the papers in front of him and the little inkpot and collection of quills set into the desk.

He's tasked with recording everything that happens. Princess Silvanie's ability to project her thoughts was strengthening almost as fast as Allay's ability to read them.

Princess Silvanie took her seat in the throne. Allay stood just a little back and to the right. Hidden behind the throne was a small table with a decanter of wine.

Did you want wine?

Not yet. I will after a few of these sessions.

Allay smirked at the image of an old lord promising he had done nothing dishonorable. The most amazing thing about all of this wasn't the lords or the beauty of the palace. It was the humor Princess Silvanie had about everything. Even the death of her parents. It wasn't as horrible as it sounded. The king and queen were busy in life and had little time for raising their children. The ones the princess had turned to for comfort when her brother died were the servants who had raised her. Her nursery maids were still there to hold her when she needed. Her father was little more than a dinner companion and her mother a tutor. She loved them and hurt for their loss, but they weren't her whole world the way Missy and Cook were for Allay.

The guards at the far end of the room snapped to attention and announced the first lord. Allay recognized the old man who entered from the council meeting. He was the one who was asleep until they

110

called his name as the next heir after Princess Silvanie. He'd thought of it as a joke then and was still laughing in his mind now. He kept the humor hidden through the formal greetings and the start of the interview.

He's thinking how proud your father would be of your ability to play the game, Allay reported when the lord looked directly at the princess.

Silvanie nodded as though that would be expected.

And now he's wondering how long it will be before he can get back to the dining room.

Silvanie smiled at that. Her own thoughts were about the silliness of this situation. Her uncle had no desire for the power he had, let alone the responsibility of running the whole country. King Thorwin kept him on the council as an excuse to let him enjoy the hospitality of the palace. A grace Silvanie planned to continue.

Sir Delare had other ideas. He pushed the old lord to account for his actions in so many situations it was a wonder Lord Charwin didn't laugh in Delare's face. Delare had to have noticed the sense of play in Lord Charwin's thoughts.

Through the whole thing, Silvanie sat silent. Her thoughts focused on the scene before her, analyzing Delare as much as Charwin. Then it was over. The lord left.

"I'll have a sip of wine now." Silvanie spoke just as Sir Delare turned to say something to her.

The next lord was announced and it all started again. Lord after lord answered Sir Delare's questions with lies and half-truths meant to prove their loyalty to King Thorwin. Their thoughts were less charitable. Many felt resentment that Princess Silvanie was to be named heir apparent the day of the assassinations. Emphasis on "princess." One after another they imagined the princess to be both incompetent and a skilled manipulator who arranged the assassination herself. Allay shared a smile with Silvanie over that irony.

This is the third time I've seen this story, Allay reported of the thoughts about Silvanie orchestrating the assassination.

It does seem to be a theme.

It's more than that. Allay remembered the exact thoughts of the three lords who had this theory in mind for the princess. *It's not just similar thoughts, but the same ones. I don't think they are original.*

Mind control? The thought came filled with enough fear to make Allay's heart start racing.

More like they are remembering a story.

Princess Silvanie nodded, her thoughts turning to Sir Delare and his failure to chase the story. She began to question her choice to have him run the investigation.

Every lord interviewed that day had the same story. Some put more faith in it than others. Without exception, they questioned the princess' legitimacy to rule, though most put that question in the fact that she was a woman. Sir Delare never touched the story that Silvanie was the mastermind, even when the lord's words hinted at it. By the end of the day, Allay had her own questions about Sir Delare's loyalty.

Kayla would be a more loyal investigator.

CHAPTER TWENTY-FOUR
Lord Corawin Tromadin

Corawin glared at the poor page assigned to bring him to the audience chamber for his interview with Sir Delare. Part of him knew it wasn't the page's fault, but he had no one else to glare at. Not to mention it was fun watching the kid squirm. This boy would never make it to squire, let alone knight, if he didn't learn to use his backbone.

"Lord Corawin Tromadin," the guard bellowed when the door to the audience chamber opened.

The room was empty of the usual courtiers who decorated the chamber. It should have been empty of all except the clerk and Delare, but the princess and her pet were there as well. Worse than that, the princess sat on the throne as though it were already hers.

"Your Majesty." Corawin bowed. He couldn't afford to be seen as anything less than loyal, though it chaffed.

She inclined her head in acceptance but said nothing. At least she had learned that from her little pet. The pet didn't acknowledge him at all. That was a little off, but then she was Silvanie's pet. A dog should only obey its master after all.

"Lord Tromadin." Sir Delare bowed only half as deep as he should have. "How is your special hunt?"

Why of all things would he start with that? "My men are still tracking her."

"Ah, I see." Delare kept his face plastered with that annoying grin of his. "I wouldn't think a sick woman would be all that difficult to track."

"Her sickness appears to be in her head rather than her body."

Corawin cast about for an explanation that would make sense and get them off this topic. "The green tint is from a dye we found in her home."

Delare nodded. "Well, I hope you find her soon."

Then came the real questions. Where was he during the public appearance? What had he been doing prior to that? How much time did he really spend looking for his green peasant?

The point seemed obvious. How loyal had he been to the late King Thorwin and how loyal would he be to the princess should she become queen? There was no point in lying about it now. He was upset with the king's decision to name his daughter as heir. There was no precedent to think a queen would be able to run the country as well as a king. Besides, Silvanie didn't have the training or experience to make a good leader.

"Had King Thorwin lived, she would have received that training," Delare suggested.

"Had he lived or not, a prince would have been trained in governance from the time he could walk. A princess, on the other hand, was taught to plan parties and run a household."

The pet reacted to that statement, and Silvanie gave a small shake of her head. So the pet was listening. Maybe Callay was right to think there was more than just master and servant going on.

"Isn't running a country a lot like running a household?" Delare pressed on.

"Not in the least. The scale is something completely different. Then there are the neighbors to think of. A household doesn't need to fear invasion from the next house over. A country does."

More reaction from the pet. This time Silvanie leaned back a bit in her chair. Something was going on between those two.

"My lord?" Delare moved to block his view of the princess. "I must ask you to focus. We need to get through this so you can get back to your duties."

"Then get on with it."

Delare continued. Now they were all about County Tromadin. How many villages? Were they in danger of invasion by County Farthingay? Of all the stupid notions. Corawin answered with as little detail as the man would let him get away with. A county was a lord's kingdom. He should be able to run it however he sees fit. The profits or lack thereof need be the only rebuke to a poor leader.

In order to keep a county functioning properly, a lord had to balance between discipline and the illusion of choice for the peasants. As long as the peasants think they have a choice, they are more willing to accept the punishments that come from not performing to expectation. He taught his sons as much, bringing them along to witness the proper way to keep a town in line.

He never dealt directly with any individual peasant; that would be beneath his station. He gave his orders to their chosen leader and let the leader hand out punishments. Except of course in those cases where the law of the country said it was his responsibility to hand down judgment, as in murder or theft of community property. That was the proper answer, so that was the one he gave. The truth about how Corawin handled the towns in his county that were unable to pay their taxes didn't need to be told to this man or in front of those girls. They wouldn't understand.

At that moment, the pet chose to hand Silvanie a wine goblet. There it was again. The timing of the little things, just as Callay—damn that man—had said meant something.

"Just one last thing." Delare was still grinning at him. "Who do you think is best to run this country?"

That was a dangerous question. He couldn't play it off a joke like he had at the reception with the other lords. Give his true opinion and they would be sure he'd hired the assassin. If he said Charwin, they'd know he was lying, and he couldn't bring himself to name Silvanie.

"Lord Callay, though I know he's too far down the succession to take the throne." Corawin threw them a bone. "He may seem like a schemer, but he's quite capable of choosing the best course of action from the list of possibilities. He has the charm to keep people happy and the discipline to keep them in line."

"An interesting choice," Sir Delare said. "Is there anything else you'd like to tell us?"

"No," Corawin snapped. "Thank you."

This whole process was a farce. One that took more than an hour out of his morning. He had conversations to manipulate and ideas to plant. He was expecting a report from his men, who were scouring the city looking for that green-skinned freak of a demon the priests claimed fit his requirements.

"Lord Tromadin?" Callay stepped out of a window nook overlooking the palace garden.

"Hello." Corawin slowed just enough for Callay to catch up.

"Have you heard?"

"About what?"

"The demon was seen leaving the city, but not by the gates." Callay was too cheerful about this.

"What, did she fly over the wall?"

"Climbed it actually. Seems she's made friends of the gutter snipes."

That explained Callay's cheeriness. "So a demon likes little kids without homes. What's news about that?"

"Not so much that, but rather the direction she was heading." He just about bounced with joy. "Right back toward Lake Thorn and beyond to Tromadin County."

"Oh bloody stars." Corawin all but ran for the palace entrance. That demon was going to kill him if he didn't get to her first.

CHAPTER TWENTY-FIVE
Kayla

Kayla found Marissa's hut exactly where Missy told her it would be. What Missy hadn't warned her about were the gardens. All around the little hut were beautifully maintained gardens with just about every plant Kayla had seen except trees growing in them. Between the gardens were equally well-maintained paths. The paths twisted and turned every which way, ending in little coves all through the gardens. Despite plenty of evidence that others cut through the gardens to get to the door, Kayla chose to stay on the paths. Her people didn't keep gardens, but the Krinna did. She learned from them the importance of keeping the plants safe and undisturbed.

Krinna gardens were filled with plants that couldn't grow naturally in the northern regions where the Krinna lived, but were essential for the Krinna's medicine. Stepping in one of their gardens could mean the death of one of their children in the cold season. She didn't know the plants here, but she wasn't going to take the chance that any of them were as vital as a Krinna garden.

It took her over an hour to work her way through all the paths and reach the front of the little cottage. As she came around the corner of the little hut, she found a woman standing in the doorway.

"Well, this is a first," the woman said with a smile. "No one has ever walked the whole maze without cheating at least once."

Kayla nodded to the woman. "I assume the plants are precious or you wouldn't care for them."

The woman laughed. "You are more a stranger than I expected. I'm Marissa, local herb woman. What brings you all the way to the center of my maze?"

"I'm Kayla, and a woman named Missy suggested you might be able to help me."

Marissa leaned harder into the side of the doorway. "That would be the Missy who runs the Broken Ale?"

Kayla nodded.

"It was Missy, not Addy, who told you of me."

Kayla nodded again. "If by Addy you mean the woman who is called Cook."

Marissa's eyes darkened. Kayla wished she knew the whole history between these women.

"You'd best come in. Do you drink tea?"

Kayla convinced Marissa that a simple glass of water was all she needed. Still, Marissa bustled about her little stove, making a production of steeping some tea for herself. It was hard not to notice the pain and worry radiating from her.

"There is only one topic that would have Missy sending you to me. What do you want with that bastard Callay?"

Kayla smiled. "I need to find a scandal."

Marissa looked at her over the teacup. "You've come for the right lord." She set the cup back on its saucer without drinking. "There are as many scandals in that lord's house as there are stars in the sky. Finding one will be easy. Getting it to stick is the trick."

So Kayla had learned on her journey through Callay County. All she had to do when the peasants held their pitchforks in fear was ask for stories about Callay. Suddenly, the people were more than happy to talk to her. She learned how often the lord failed to send in his taxes and blamed the peasants for it. They were forced to give double, leaving barely enough to keep them through the cold season. She learned of a custom called "first night" where the lord took a bride from her husband on the night of their wedding. There were other abuses as well, all of them horrifying.

Kayla promised every village she passed through that she would avenge them. All she needed were some of his victims to return with her to Greylein. That was where her mission failed every time. They were willing to tell a demon their story, but anyone who had actual power to do anything about it scared them.

"Naturally," Marissa said. "Would you talk to someone else called 'lord' if you had been through what they have?"

Kayla started to say yes. It was like the Magisters in Kralt. They had the whole population convinced that magic without the training they had was dangerous. So dangerous that people deliberately avoided

118

trying to do magic unless they could pay for the training. Magic wasn't that hard to control, and it didn't take so much effort to learn it should be locked away where most people would never have access. But the people believed so they never tried.

"Will you come?"

Marissa shook her head. "I would, but I don't have the kind of story you need."

"Do you know someone who does?"

"I know a lot of people." Marissa let her head fall. "And the one who has the best story of all, if you can get to her. Callay's own daughter would turn against him in heartbeat if she ever got the chance. You can't get a bigger scandal than that."

"Why does she hate him so?"

Marissa smiled. "I'll let her tell you. It's her story." Marissa was up and moving again, this time cleaning everything she'd touched in making her tea. "We'll have to wait a bit. It will be easier to get in when the guards are getting hungry." She chattered on about having to be careful about who sees them walking together. And wondering what she could bring as an appropriate gift to a hostess who was receiving unexpected guests.

Kayla pulled her feet up into the chair to stay out of the way as much as possible. She would have asked to help, but she was afraid that would be more in the way than anything. She watched as a basket was filled with jars and pouches then covered with an embroidered cloth. A similar cloth landed on Kayla's chest.

"Cover your face with that." Marissa moved with the same speed and purpose Cook used when she was upset. Efficient yet all over the place. "And your hands too." A pair of gloves landed in her lap. "Do you know anything about healing?"

"I can close a gaping wound."

"Close enough." Marissa stood ready by the door. She wore a hooded cloak similar to the one Kayla used to conceal her features and carried the basket that was now full of dried herbs and jars of ointments or preserves.

Kayla pulled on the gloves and wrapped the cloth around her face before pulling up the hood to further conceal her.

"Now, let me teach you the shortest way through my gardens."

Kayla's long legs gave her an advantage of speed compared with most humans. With Marissa, she struggled to keep up.

"Now, our game is going to be Lady Callay's deepest desire, which is to restore her daughter to health. I'll introduce you as a foreign witch, so don't say anything." Marissa chattered on about the plan and how they were going to weasel their way into see Avianna and get time alone with her to talk about Kayla's plan.

Kayla wasn't sure she had a plan but didn't find a pause to say so. She let Marissa tell her about everything except what happened to Avianna to convince her father that locking her away was better than marrying her out to create alliances. Another custom Kayla found abhorrent. She added it to the list of things to bring up with Silvanie.

"Here we are. We're peasants, so we'll have to enter through the kitchen."

"I thought we were healers."

"We are, but that still makes us servants." Marissa led the way to the small door next to the garden.

"Healers should be more respected than this," Kayla grumbled. She thought of the Krinna again. Their most revered members of the community were the ones who tended the sick and wounded.

"Shh." Marissa cautioned. She knocked on the door.

Kayla tried not to laugh at the grumbling from the other side of the door before it opened. It sounded almost exactly like Cook whenever she was interrupted in the preparation of a meal. The woman who opened the door looked nothing like her. Where Cook was muscular, this woman was fat. Cook's long hair was a dark brown; this woman had her rust-colored hair cut short.

"Ah, Marissa, how do you always know when we are up to our ears in problems?"

"Because I know your problems." Marissa hugged the woman. "I've brought you something." She pulled a jar out of the basket.

"Is that…?"

"You know it is. We've come to see the mistress."

"Lady Callay isn't here."

"Then we'll just head up on our own."

The cook shook her head. "The lady took the key with her. Poor girl, there's only so much we can push through the slot in the door."

"We'll go up anyway. My friend won't be here tomorrow." Marissa pushed past the large woman, pulling Kayla along with her. "There are more treats in the basket." She dropped the basket on the kitchen table.

They went up a small set of stairs that wound around the inside of one of the towers. At the top was a door with a small window in it.

"Avianna?" Marissa called.

"Marissa?" a weak voice called back. "It's so good to hear you."

"I've brought a friend."

120

There was a moment of silence. "I'm not to see anyone. Father sent a letter."

Kayla could feel power running through the clasp on the door. The lock was made of copper, how lucky. She grabbed hold of the power and pushed. The door swung open.

Marissa stared at her with wide-eyed amazement.

"I have a key." Kayla smiled back before she realized her face was still covered in the embroidered cloth.

"How did you get a key?" the girl inside asked.

"I made it." Kayla followed Marissa into the room.

The girl sitting there was light-skinned, with her long brown hair pulled back in a simple braid. Her dress appeared simple as well, though well made. Her hands clutched a pair of sticks with yarn twined around them, flowing off down her lap. She didn't look around when Kayla approached.

"I haven't heard your voice before," Avianna said. "You must be from far away."

"Farther than I can describe," Kayla admitted.

She finally got a look at Avianna's face. There were jagged scars all around her eyes that prevented Kayla from noticing anything else. The eyes themselves were clouded over.

At Marissa's urging, Avianna explained how her father had ordered his men to beat her blind. It had started when he caught her with a serving maid in a compromising position. He'd slit the throat of her lover right in front of her with his own hand. Then he made sure that was the last sight she saw.

"That is…" Kayla had to force herself to drop her claws. She'd found them in her hands several times throughout the story. "How can you people live like this?"

Marissa's face had gone hard, and Avianna dropped her head.

"You let the circumstances of your birth decide who your leaders are rather than any kind of skill. You think you can't leave when things are going bad. What would happen if the peasants who do all the work just got up a left?" Kayla paced the short distance between the walls of the room.

"I'd leave this life in an instant if I could just see the way," Avianna shot back. "Show me how I can leave."

"Come with me to Greylein," Kayla said. "Show them what kind of man your father really is."

"What good would that do? They're all the same."

"And they're all ashamed of it." Kayla caught a hint of what the game was really all about. "Your father keeps you hidden, so the best way to get back at him is to show you off to the world."

"No." She hid her face in her hands. "I can't let them see me like this."

Kayla knelt in front of the girl and pulled her hands away. "If I can let them see my green skin and demon ears, you can show off your beauty."

Avianna put her hands on Kayla's face and explored all the shapes that were different from a human. "You're a demon?"

"Not where I'm from." Kayla let Avianna continue to explore her face.

Marissa stood near the door with her arms crossed over her stomach. She spent as much time looking into the narrow stairway as watching Kayla and Avianna. "I could talk you up here, but we are going to have a much harder time getting her out of here," Marissa said. "I can't ask my friends to put themselves in that kind of danger."

"Getting out is easy." Kayla opened a portal to her room at the Broken Ale. She also pushed the lock back into place.

Kayla stood and took Avianna's hand. Avianna put her sticks and yarn on the chair behind her when she stood. "Are you a priest?" Avianna asked.

"No."

"I can hear the hum of the gods around you."

"Just trust me." Kayla waved for Marissa to lead them through the portal.

CHAPTER TWENTY-SIX
Lord Corawin Tromadin

Corawin sat at his desk, glaring across at Brace. "What did you say?"

"Sir, the only information we have on the demon comes from the street children." Brace stood as bold as ever across from him. "They say she is Star Born."

"Star Born are myths." Corawin slammed his hand on the table. This was getting out of hand, the rumors and myths growing up around that demon.

"We know that, sir, but these are children." Brace lifted his shoulders. "They believe."

They were undisciplined children from wayward parents who couldn't be bothered to properly train them. "Fine, what do these... children say of the Star Born?"

Brace sighed. "They say she is going to bring light to all the dark places."

"What is that supposed to mean?"

"I wish I knew, sir," Brace said. "They also said she travels south to find a star."

South wasn't County Tromadin. What could the demon be looking for in the south?

"Tromadin!" Callay burst into his office, face red and fists balled.

A step behind him came the butler bowing in fear. Corawin waved the butler off while glaring at his fellow lord. Some familiarity was expected between peers, but this was rude.

"If you don't get that damned demon of yours under control I'll—"

"You'll what?" Corawin stood. "You'll tell everyone that I called her? And I'll show them you financed it."

Callay stopped short, still huffing. "I'll tell them what really happened to Georgi."

Corawin caught his breath. He hadn't thought of his middle son in years. It took him a moment to remember the truth Callay spoke of separate from the story he'd spread to explain the death.

"No need to get so personal." Corawin stepped around the desk. "Let's not forget your precious Avianna."

Callay stood his ground. "That's not much of a threat anymore. Your demon took her and the rest of the household."

Took them? Corawin couldn't imagine what that demon would do with that many peasants. "How do you know she took them?"

"She was seen, you idiot." Callay brought his chest within inches of Corawin's "She was seen all the way from here to my home. How is it your men can't track her when she sticks out like a sore thumb. Worse than that, she's been talking to the peasants. Talking. Like she pretended she didn't know what we were saying at the ceremony; now she's talking to the damned peasants."

"Get a rein on yourself, man." Corawin took a step back. "You sound like a lunatic."

There was a way to swing this to his advantage if he could just think for a moment. The demon was known now, and everyone saw its effects at the naming ceremony. They didn't know it, but they saw it.

"Silvanie has been with the demon and come back," Corawin said. "She's been corrupted, obviously."

"What are you talking about?"

"The demon," Corawin said. "Now listen, we called her to kill the royals so we could take power, right?"

Callay rolled his eyes.

"It didn't work out that way, but this could be better." Corawin strode across the room. Oh, yes, this was much better.

"You aren't making any sense." Callay stood back.

"You aren't listening." Corawin turned to face the other lord. "That demon has corrupted the princess. She's not fit to rule. And the same can be said of any who oppose us."

"But they haven't all seen the demon. It's not like she's kidnapped them all and brought them back." Callay shook his head.

"But they all have times they can't or won't account for." Corawin loved this idea. Any of them could have been corrupted by the demon with that logic. Any of them except him."

"You've been chasing her across the land." Callay pointed a finger directly at Corawin. "They'll use that as proof against us."

"I chase her because I know her for what she is." Oh, this was going to be a great story. Spin it right and this story could carry him through his entire reign. "Don't you get it? Demons can change shape to make you think you are talking to an innocent child or your own mother, if that's what it takes to get you to do what it wants."

"They can? I thought that was just a story."

Corawin rolled his eyes. "It is just a story. Every bit as much of a story as that funeral you held for Avianna."

Callay finally caught on. "As long as they believe it, it's true."

"There's so much more to plan for something like this." Corawin's mind was ablaze. He hadn't had this much fun since planning his takeover of Tromadin County. There were so many details to get right so it wouldn't fall back on him. In this case, there was also the side issue of Callay. That lord needed to be out of the picture before Corawin took the throne.

"Of course, so what's the plan?" Callay was as eager as ever to get in on the plan, now that he saw it as a plan.

"For now, spread the word that your household was taken by the demon. Play up how scared you are that the demon is targeting you." Corawin could feel this plan taking shape. It would land him on the throne within a month. And Callay would be a washed-up old lunatic.

"What are you going to do?"

"Make it look like I've been targeted too." Corawin lied. He ushered Callay out of his office.

"Sir, you know this plan could backfire on you with disastrous effects." Brace stayed in the corner where he'd hidden through the whole conversation.

Corawin swore he would teach that man to show some respect someday. "Any plan worth attempting has that danger."

"Perhaps." He stepped out of the shadow. "What is my part in this plan?"

"Same as it was before." Corawin sat at the desk. "Find that demon and kill her. Only, try not to make a spectacle of it. I need people to think she's still out there somewhere." He pulled out a sheet of paper. "And if you get the chance, talk about how silly the kids are to believe a demon could be Star Born."

"Sir?"

"No one wants to be seen as a silly child, do they?"

Brace nodded. Whether he understood or not, he'd obey. Corawin would bet he understood far more than he let on. That could be a danger as well.

CHAPTER TWENTY-SEVEN
Kayla

Kayla put the finishing touches on Avianna's decorations. It made her scars look more like butterfly wings and distracted from the foggy eyes themselves. She helped her into the fancy dress Missy found for them.

"Are you ready?" Kayla asked.

Avianna nodded her head. "You'll be there with me?"

"Of course. Never far from your side." Kayla opened the portal to the little room where she had waited during the council meeting so many days ago.

The room hadn't changed from how she remembered it. Gold and silver pressed into the walls in a looping design. Four high-backed chairs sat in a curve around the small fireplace that was unlit today. There were pedestals around the room with decorated bowls and vases set on them. Only now, some of them were made of copper.

Kayla drank in the power that was still barely a trickle. She wondered if it was a bad sign that she was getting used to the lack of power available here. Already she'd improved her efficiency with the portals so they didn't take as much from her as they had. She learned to use the power sparingly, relying as much as possible on her other skills.

I'm so happy to see you. Allay ran through the door, forgetting all she'd learned of grace and manners in the royal house. She wrapped herself around Kayla so tight. *I need to know what you think about so many things.*

We'll have to talk later. Kayla hugged the girl back. *For now I need you to help me introduce my friend.*

Allay's amazement when she looked at Avianna dripped off of her like sweat on a hot day. *She's so pretty.*

"Allay?" Silvanie stood near the door.

Sorry. Lady Kayla to see you, with a friend. Allay bowed herself out of the way.

"Your Majesty." Kayla nodded her head. She'd also learned some of the customs of this land, even when she found them silly. "I'd like to present Lady Avianna Callay."

"Impossible." Silvanie stared at Avianna with an intensity that would have made the girl nervous had she seen it.

"Silvanie?" Kayla asked. "How is this impossible? She's the daughter of Lord Callay."

"Lady Avianna Callay died three years ago. I was at her funeral."

"I'm not dead," Avianna whined. "He said I was dead? He held a funeral?" Her breathing became erratic while her hand reached out for Kayla.

Kayla shot a glare at Silvanie before pulling Avianna into a comforting hug. "You aren't dead. This is just another of your father's tricks."

Allay came to help guide the now sobbing Avianna to a chair.

"Listen to her story before you decide something is impossible." Kayla directed her words to Silvanie, though she was done with playing at being polite.

"How dare you speak to me like that?"

Kayla stood to her full height, leaving Allay to calm Avianna. "I am not your subject."

"Then leave."

"I'd love to."

"Gua—"

Kayla pounced, backing Silvanie to the wall with a claw at her throat. "Now listen carefully, princess. What happened to your parents is a result of this sense of entitlement you and all the lords share. You won't be a great leader just because you were born to be one. You have to listen to the people around you and convince them you are a great leader."

"Stop, please." Avianna gasped.

Kayla could see Allay was lending the girl her eyes. That was a new trick.

"Silvanie, please listen to her." Avianna turned Allay's eyes to Silvanie. "Do you remember that time when we were young and careless? We snuck down to the kitchens to try to get some sweets but stumbled across the servant's bath instead?"

Silvanie nodded slightly.

"I never forgot what we saw. You were disgusted and never wanted to talk about it, but I was curious."

Silvanie stiffened where she stood.

"I could never talk about it with any of our peers. They wouldn't understand. Besides, the wailing about marriages was already beginning. I had to talk about it to someone. One of the serving girls knew exactly what I meant. We tried so many things, and even though I knew it could never be, I found happiness in her arms. We knew how important it was to keep it hidden. But we were careless one day and Father found out."

Kayla turned away for the rest of the story. Even knowing what was coming, the sound of it made her stomach tighten. This wasn't the way a family should work. Families were the people who protected you from this kind of horror. They were the ones you would choose to live the rest of your life with.

"This isn't true," Silvanie whispered. "It can't be true."

It's true. Allay stood next to Avianna. *You ask me to look into everyone's thoughts and tell you what I find. You ask me to look into the minds of all those men in the council of lords and I show you the disgusting things I see there. Don't you dare distrust me now.*

"Leave us, both of you." Silvanie's voice rose barely above a whisper but was filled with venom.

Allay dropped to one knee before heading for the door. Kayla followed without acknowledging Silvanie's rank. She had her hood in place before the guards saw her. Their surprise was still palpable. Kayla wasn't in the mood to be challenged by them, so she walked with all the speed her legs could manage to the next corner.

She willed herself invisible while she waited for Allay to catch up.

Are you trying to get on the princess' bad side?

No. Kayla wasn't sure she needed the princess now. Not with the way things were panning out. *I'm trying to do whatever it takes to get home.*

And she's trying to do the same.

Even seeing the thoughts in Allay's head, it was hard to believe. Kayla shook her head and started walking again.

Wait, please don't leave again.

Kayla slowed to Allay's pace. *I'm not welcome here. The guards would probably attack if they knew what I am. Even Silvanie...*

Allay grabbed Kayla's arm and pulled her to a stop. *If you let them know you, they wouldn't attack you.*

There were images in Allay's mind of the way the other servants treated her the first days she was here and how she managed to make some of them accept her. There were also images of the guards granting special privileges to favored servants.

It's all about letting people know who you really are.

Kayla shook her head. *For the servants, that may be true, but for Silvanie and the lords and all the ones who think they have power, it's a game. A game about appearances over actual substance. They worry about how things will look, not whether it's right or wrong. I can't be a part of this game.*

Allay let go and stepped back. Her mind shut Kayla out completely while her eyes filled with tears. Then she turned and fled back the way they'd come.

Kayla watched her go. She had to believe it was for the best. Allay needed friends of her own world, not some alien demon who would jump through the first portal to home that presented itself. She shouldn't care about the political system of a place that would only be a bad dream just as soon as she could figure a way to wake up. Until then, she had to play along only enough to get back to Kralt and Jarron and home. Making friends here would only hamper her real goal.

She'd done it Silvanie's way, starting with the lesser of the lords. The one who took orders rather than gave them. It was time she turned her attention to the greater of the lords. The one whose land she'd been called to. Lord Corawin Tromadin, lord of County Tromadin and the biggest horned beast she'd ever dealt with.

More like run from. She was done running. She'd learned enough about her prey to know he was dangerous when he felt he was in control. He was a lord and that meant he would treat his people with contempt. Those same people who made his way of life possible. It was time to take his people away from him.

CHAPTER TWENTY-EIGHT
Allay

Allay ran through the open halls of the palace, not caring that she was supposed to keep herself hidden. She did use the servant's gate to leave the palace grounds only because it was closer to the Temple of Odran. Even in the city streets, she ran, slipping through the crowd the way only a child can. She arrived out of breath.

Through the gasping breaths, she bowed to the four directions, thinking the words of the wayfarer's prayer. Most people muttered their way through the prayer, so no one noticed she didn't speak at all. The priests said it was more important to understand the prayer than speak it properly.

Odran was the god Missy chose when it was time for Allay to be assessed for magic potential, though she was pledged to Kethry. The priests spent three days just trying to figure out how to conduct the tests. She stayed in the temple three more days while they prayed and tested her. All the while she learned how to be a priest of Odran from their thoughts. She'd prayed they wouldn't find her capable of magic. She wanted to go home to Missy and Cook. She'd wondered often if she'd hidden her ability just so they wouldn't keep her in the temple.

Supposedly, it was the god who did the tests, and gods could see everything. So if she had been able to hide her magic potential, it was because Odran himself allowed it.

Allay waited until her breath returned to normal before approaching the prayer wheel. She lay her hand on the symbol that looked like a sun radiating in all directions. The symbol of wisdom.

I need to know if what I'm doing is right. She thought the words carefully to be sure he would understand. Three times she played the words through her mind, then pushed the wheel around three times as well, careful to only touch the sun.

She stepped away from the wheel so others would be able to make their requests of the god. She found a kneeling pad and dropped to the position she saw the priests take when they were supposed to be communing with Odran.

It has been so long since I have heard your heart.

Allay wanted to look around to see who had spoken, but she knew she wouldn't see. She squeezed her eyes tighter to stop the temptation.

I haven't had questions like this. She tried to make her confusion clear.

You have had many problems and many sources of wisdom. Images of the men who thought her old enough to play with and those on the street not quite adults and no longer children who pushed and picked at anyone they could. She also saw the griffins gathering the wood for her. Missy and Cook filled her mind as well. They were both problems and wisdom in the images.

Nothing like this. She thought of Kayla. How she was the first to accept her mind voice and teach her to use it with Missy and Cook. She thought of the way Kayla had been pulled by priests at the request of a lord from her world to this.

They were my priests, in name if not conviction.

Allay stiffened. How could priests not believe in the god they were to care for? How could Odran have lent them the power to do what they did to Kayla?

For you, my dear. And Silvanie, her face appeared in Allay's mind. *And all the others she will help before she finds her way home.* Many faces appeared before her. Some she knew, but most were complete strangers. Hundreds of them, maybe thousands. Not all of them human.

But what of her life before? Allay thought of the images Kayla had shown her of Jarron and all the children they were in charge of.

They will be stronger for this interruption as well. There are times when we must do things that are hard to make the changes that are needed.

Allay wished that weren't true. She couldn't call the god a liar, though.

So you will send her back?

I am not the one preventing her from returning to her world. A man with skin as black as soot appeared wrapped in strands of purple light. Those lines were a kind of power, like all the colors she'd seen through Crystal's eyes. Allay knew this man to be evil beyond the horrible things

132

she'd seen in the minds of the council lords.

Who is that? What is he?

I cannot tell you. Even this will be clear only with time. With that thought came the understanding that even the god did not know. That filled her with fear. What kind of evil could walk in the light and still be unknown to the gods?

Allay felt this might be the end of the conversation. She wasn't a priest who could command the attention of Odran for long prayers. Still, she had to ask, *Why don't I have a voice?*

My pet, you have the loudest voice in the known realms. It is your voice that will change the course of history.

Then he was gone. Everything he said began to fade from her mind. All the images blurred in her memory.

"Hush child, hush." A young woman in priest's robes was lowering her onto the floor. "Don't fight it. You'll remember the important part."

Allay looked up at her in confusion. What was she talking about?

"You need to sleep." The woman waved to someone Allay couldn't see. "It's hard the first time he talks directly to you, and you didn't have any training."

I've been training all my life. Allay pushed the words directly into the woman's head.

The priest almost dropped her with the surprise. Allay felt the familiarity of her voice in the priest's mind. Her voice came like the voice of the god to the priest. That must have been what he meant when he said, "You have the loudest voice in the known realms."

That was all she remembered. The exhaustion began to win against her will to remain conscious just as another priest, a man, came to help the woman lift her from the floor.

"What happened?" the man asked.

"She spoke to Odran," the woman answered in awed tones.

"How?"

Allay didn't hear the answer.

CHAPTER TWENTY-NINE
Kayla

"I'm not surprised." Marissa spoke quietly as she led Kayla through the streets of the city. "Princess Silvanie is as much a lord as any of them."

Kayla didn't know why she had returned to the Broken Ale after her failed mission to stir up a scandal with Avianna Callay. Marissa decided it must have been so they could spend the day shopping among the crafters of the capital city. So here they were. Kayla covered as best she could in the heat of the day while Marissa lead her from street to street, seeking the things that didn't often come her way with the traveling merchants that supplied the outlying villages.

"Wouldn't that mean Avianna is also one of them? Yet she was willing to speak against her father." Kayla felt the pull of power as they entered the blacksmith's quarter.

"Perhaps she was before." Marissa shrugged. "But then her lover was killed; she was blinded and hidden away. That will have an effect on a person."

Kayla nodded. She looked around. There were always small pockets of power, usually in the pouches of coins people carried. This feeling was different. It was strong enough to call her, almost like home. At home, the power pulled in every direction. Here, it pulled her farther down the lane between stone built kilns.

"You did what you could. Leave it to them to finish making a scandal." Marissa stopped to inspect an iron cauldron.

Kayla sighed. "The scandal was supposed to give me the opportunity to go home." All it did was take time. That and teach her more about the demons who lived in this world.

"Of course." Marissa smiled at her. "What do you think of this one?"

The cauldron was solid and smooth. "I thought you had one just like it."

Marissa shook her head. "The one I have is becoming pock-marked. It's getting harder to ensure I don't contaminate my potions with each other."

"I promise you, this cauldron will not pock for years to come." A man whose pink skin was hidden behind soot came up to them. "Can I assume you are an herb woman?" He smiled at Marissa.

"You can." Marissa smiled back.

Kayla watched them flirt about the cauldron for a few moments before the real issues started to come out. Marissa proved herself to be a skilled negotiator, using all the perceptions he had about her to wheedle more concessions from him. It was like watching Jarron negotiate with a vendor. She was just starting to convince him that she couldn't buy it if he couldn't find some way to get it to her house, when Kayla decided to seek the source of power.

She closed her eyes to focus on the direction of the power. When she opened them, she was facing the brick wall of an iron furnace. Of course, power didn't care about the streets or structures of the world. It took will to force the power to affect the physical world. She stepped into the street, keeping her focus on the power. She wove through the crowds on the street, paying more attention to shadows than forms to keep her face hidden and her mind focused.

Three forges down, between a pair of weapon makers, she found a smaller forge focused on art more than function. There were decorative vases and bowls lining the little shop where others had pots or swords. Other pieces were purely decorative, with no obvious function. Through everything, between each piece and the next, the power danced. It danced within her as well.

In this place, she could almost feel like she was home.

"I wondered when you would show up." A demon like all the rest in the shops and forges of this section smiled at her.

Kayla took half a step back into a ready stance. "Why would you expect me here?"

He laughed. "You are Kethry's angel. She told us you would need us."

Another man emerged from the shadows at the back of the forge. This one was as different as you could get from all the others save the soot that coated his skin. He was short, thin, with no defined

136

muscles. He moved as though touching the ground were optional. He smiled as well, though his was more of a turning up at the corners of his lips than a grin.

"Who is Kethry?"

Both men laughed. The little one spoke with a voice to match his stature. "She's a child if you look at her only with your eyes. Someone named her for the god of compassion, and someday they'll get her into a temple and find she's a lot more than just a little girl."

"She told us about you and said we should make a place for the angel," the larger one said. "So we added a chair right over there."

There was a chair, simple and beautiful, in the corner. It was made of copper with spaces all around for water. The chair glowed with power. Kayla wanted to run to it, sit in it, and feel the power all around her, but she held back. There were motivations at work here that she couldn't trace or understand.

"Why would this Kethry tell you about me?"

"Please, come sit." The smaller man faded back toward the chair. "We can explain as much as we know over tea." He pulled out two copper teapots. One marked clearly for her.

The larger man smiled. "She also brought us a tea she says comes all the way from Crystal in her mountain lair." He also moved toward the copper chair, pulling out a small wood table and a couple of stools. "She warned us not to taste it, though."

The smaller man added steaming water from a kettle near the forge to both pots, and Kayla could smell the leaves of the Hedgelock plant. A plant so deadly simply touching it could kill a demon. Kayla found it delicious. The scent from the second pot was the normal earthy smell of the tea Cook and Missy served in the morning.

Temptation overcame suspicion and she joined them. Deeper in the shop, the swirls of power embraced her, weakening her resolve to keep herself separate from the people of this world. If there were places like this, she could live here. That thought alone scared her. Could she really abandon Jarron, the kids, and her family so easily for a small refuge in an otherwise hostile world?

No, you can take the time to do what you need to do.

The thought came from somewhere deep within her mind and yet wasn't hers. Kayla dropped into a fighting stance, looking in every direction for the source of the voice.

"Be still," a small girl in the dirt-covered rags of the street said. "You do not need to worry here."

Kayla had seen her before. The day of the assassination, when the street children showed her how to get to the rooftops. "Kethry?"

The girl giggled and bowed. Her smile was bright in a way that wasn't quite real. Then she ran off, disappearing into the crowd before Kayla could think of anything else to say.

"We really don't understand all that much ourselves," the larger man said. His name was Dan, and he had been denied by his family for choosing Allan as his partner.

Kayla didn't know where the knowledge came from.

"Tell me what you do know," Kayla said, smiling to match theirs as best she could. This couldn't get any weirder, and she would probably need full power soon. She sat in the chair and let the power surround her as though she were lying on a sun-warmed hill in the steppe of her home.

"There are changes coming." Allan poured the tea. "Many of us who were almost kept by the temples have felt it for years. Neither the priests nor the normals feel it the way we do."

"Almost kept by the temples?"

Dan explained how every child was taken to the temples in their fifth year to be tested for magic. Most of the time, the tests are clear. Allan took up the story. Sometimes, though, the tests are not so clear. It can take days before the priests decide that child doesn't have magic and returns the child to their parents. Those children are often seen as a disappointment. Dan took the story back. Because the parents got their hopes up when the priests insisted on keeping the child for more days. These children were considered rejected by most. Among themselves, they were god-touched.

"I can feel it." Allan leaned in to tell her in a hushed tone, "I know there are big changes coming."

"Like Silvanie taking the throne?" Kayla asked.

"That's just the start." He set his tea carefully on the table with a side-glance at Dan. "There will be great changes that will reorder most of what we know to be true." His arms reached out in great arcs that could have been disastrous had he forgotten to set the tea down. "Houses will be taken down and the people will rise to make this country new."

Dan moved the teapots out of the way.

"I knew it was starting weeks ago. Then Kethry came to tell me you were here." He turned to face Kayla with eyes filled with fire. "It is you, not Silvanie, who will bring the change. You will change her as much as the rest of the world."

Kayla leaned back in the chair, pulling its power around her like a shield against the intensity of Allan's conviction.

"I'm not the hero you take me for."

Dan put his hand out to calm Allan. "We don't expect you to be a hero." Dan's look was just as intense, though he kept the intensity within him. "Heroes always do what is good and fall on that sword in the end. We only expect you will make changes that can't be ignored."

She didn't see the difference but smiled anyway. "I'll do what it takes to get home. Nothing more, nothing less."

They both leaned back with a sigh and a knowing nod to each other. They picked up their tea and sipped it again. Kayla joined them in that. Sip, sip, sip.

"You'll need to talk to the people of County Tromadin." Allan sipped again. "They are the ones who need you the most."

Kayla nodded and swallowed the last of her tea.

CHAPTER THIRTY
Kayla

The temple didn't look anything like the churches she'd seen in Kralt or the sacred places of the Krinna. If Marissa hadn't pointed it out for her, she wouldn't have known it was any different from the houses found in some areas of the city. It did stand out from the houses all around it. Where they were pushed right up to the street, with doors only two or three steps above the ground, the temple had a garden between the gate at the edge of the street and a good dozen steps up to the grand doors. The building itself was a mix of stone columns with slat boards making the walls between. It rose up from the grand doors three or four floors. The houses all around it looked like children huddling around the skirts of their mother.

Kayla hesitated at the open gate. The only time she'd been in a church, they'd run her out, claiming she had offended the resident god and should go somewhere far enough away that the lightning strike wouldn't hurt them. The lightning strike never came. The sacred realms of the Krinna were highly regulated places where she had to be escorted so she wouldn't do anything that would corrupt them. Among her own people, gods were ephemeral beings who stood in for the spirits of large groups of life forms or classes of weather when needed. Anyplace could become sacred when one needed to consult the spirits of the prey or divine the coming rains.

Everything else about the demons of this world confused her. She couldn't trust logic to tell her what to do in the temple.

"Come and be welcome." A small boy in the white robes favored by the priests of this temple bowed to her from just inside the gate.

"Am I welcome here?"

"You are expected." He stood and held out his hand. "I was chosen to bring you in." The pride in his voice made Kayla smile.

She extended her hand and let him pull her through the gate. "The mistress will tell you what you need to know. It's not hard. Follow your heart and make the people around you happy. That's the rules." He pulled her along the curving paths of the garden.

There were flowers of all colors in geometric patterns in the spaces between paths. Some she recognized from Marissa's garden and others she'd seen along the roads into Callay County. Everywhere she looked, there were people tending the plants or each other.

"The mistress is nice. I hope she will be ours for a long time to come," the boy whispered as they passed a bed of white flowers. "They say we need to be ready for her to die soon and then we will have a new mistress or master."

"Is the mistress sick?" Kayla wondered if she should have let Marissa join her here.

"No, she's just old."

They were at the stairs leading to the grand doors. The boy paused to bow his head and mouth some prayer. Kayla bowed her head as well, though she had no words to say.

"We have to go quietly." The boy took her hand again and stepped silently on the stair.

Kayla followed, placing her feet as carefully as if she were stalking a runner. Thirteen steps to the door. It opened when they were eleven steps up. The woman standing just inside was as pale as any of the demons she had seen. Her hair was as white as the robes she wore and her skin had shrunk to the size of her bones.

"Mistress Kayla?" The old woman bowed to her. "May I welcome you to the Temple of Kethry?"

"I am welcomed." Kayla bowed back but stopped halfway when she heard the boy's sudden intake of breath.

"Never mind this child. His view of the world is too stark." The old woman ruffled the boy's hair. "We must expect that you will have different customs."

The woman turned and walked into the temple. Kayla followed. Inside the temple was spare but well kept. The walls were polished to shine so the candles in globes hanging from the ceiling were able to keep back the dark. There were no carvings or paintings in the halls, though each door they passed had a sigil of some sort branded into the wood.

142

"What brings you to our temple?" the mistress asked after the second turn.

"Curiosity." Kayla looked all about trying to see what made this place sacred.

The mistress nodded. "Then you aren't here to beg to be sent home. That is good."

"Why would I beg here?" Kayla felt a bit of shock at her own answer. "It was the priests of Odran who brought me here." How did she know that? "If I were the begging sort, I'd be at their temple."

The mistress gave her an appraising look from the top of her head to her feet and back up.

"I must confess you are not what I expected."

Kayla bit back the obvious question.

They entered a large room that had the feeling of being a glade in a forest. The columns here were made of a brown stone carved smooth and reaching up to the sky above. The center of the room dipped just enough to gather any water that fell in. Opposite the door was a table filled with flowers of all colors.

"This is where we come to speak to Kethry," the mistress said. "It is easiest to hear her words when the environment is calming."

"How do you talk to Kethry?"

The mistress smiled. "We use elaborate prayers and body forms. There isn't time to teach you such things. The truth is you just have to concentrate on making your thoughts heard in the heavens and she will know what you have to say. She doesn't always answer."

"That is all you have for me?" Kayla felt she was being made a fool. "A boy who claimed he was sent for me and an old woman who is little more than an errand boy herself?"

The old woman laughed. "Child, you have no idea how nice that is to hear. I'll be here when you have questions." She retreated to a small alcove, still laughing.

Kayla turned to the table filled with flowers. *Well, here I am. I'm not sure why you've made it so clear you are taking an interest in my life.*

The air stirred around her with scents that were a breath of home.

If you are going to manipulate me through children and men who are as outcast as a street child, the least you can do is explain yourself.

"You are far more direct than any of my children." A woman stood where the table of flowers had been a moment before. She was as pink as any of the demons, with a face that curved around its features artistically.

All around the room there were subtle changes in the quality

143

of light. Shafts of sunlight she hadn't noticed before highlighted dust motes that drifted slowly in and out of shadows.

"I'm not your child."

"Of course not. You are a guest."

"I'd rather not be." Kayla let her frustration rise through her voice but forced her hands to remain open.

Kethry nodded. "Can you think of anyone you would wish this on?"

Kayla growled because there wasn't anyone she hated that much. Perhaps one of the Magisters, except they all had families as well.

"So why did it have to be me?"

"There were so many candidates." Kethry stepped forward, shifting slightly to the more angular look that was considered beauty in the cities back home. "You showed all the traits we were looking for."

"We?"

"The gods of this world."

"I know none of you," Kayla said. "Why should I care what you want?"

"Your anger is understandable."

"Then send me home." Kayla faced the woman who was looking more like her with every breath.

"I cannot." Kethry held Kayla's eyes.

"You got me here."

"We brought you here. Alone, I cannot reverse what has been done."

"Then how am I supposed to get home?"

"Reverse the evil that is plaguing our world."

"Is that a joke?" Kayla gripped her claws tighter than ever before. That much tension would make her clumsy, but she didn't plan to attack the god in front of her.

Kethry took a step back. "Your anger is understandable."

Kayla loosened her grip a bit and sank into a pounce stance. "I don't want to be understood. I want to go home."

"We mean you no harm."

"A bit late for that."

"We held off for as long as we could." Kethry moved farther back.

"It would have been better if you hadn't waited." Kayla thought of all the times she could have left and no one would have noticed.

"On the contrary, we had to allow you to formalize your relationship."

144

Kayla growled. "You waited? For that?"

Kethry raised her arms to protect herself.

"I'm done here." Kayla turned her back on the cowering god.

The room shifted back to the colors and feel it had when she first walked in. The old woman rose from her place in the alcove, but Kayla didn't wait to be escorted out.

CHAPTER THIRTY-ONE
Allay

Allay woke in her bed in the little closet off Silvanie's private rooms. Her head filled with images she could barely remember. Chasing them through her mind threatened to give her a headache, so she reluctantly let them go. What remained was a sense of peace and the knowledge she was supposed to change the world.

How was she supposed to do that?

By getting up and getting on with her duties. That was another thing. She'd gone to the temple to find out if what she was doing was right. Was she supposed to be thinking other people's private thoughts?

There was no answer to that question still. Only a feeling that she had the power to choose.

"Ah, you are up." A young maid came in. "We were worried when they brought you back from the temple."

The girl started helping Allay dress for the day. "There'll be sausage-filled muffins in the kitchen. Then you'll have to hurry. Silvanie couldn't wait for you before starting the interviews for today."

I'll go straight to the audience chamber. Allay pulled her dress up where it was supposed to be, still amazed it fit her properly.

"Don't be silly. You missed dinner last night."

Allay didn't feel hungry and the thought of sausage made her stomach tighten even further.

Maybe just some bread.

"You are trying to get me in trouble." But she smiled to take the sting out of the comment. "How about an apple? If you eat it fast, you'll be able to get to the audience chamber before anyone but Princess Silvanie notices you were late getting up."

Allay took the apple the other maid had hidden in her skirts. The maid had taken the apple for herself but would now have the chance at more of the sausage biscuits in the name of Allay. The apple was crisp and just a little tart. It sat light in her stomach as she ran through the palace halls, doing her best to stay out of the way. Still, she heard many thoughts about how strange it was to have her in the palace.

It was strange. Allay was raised to the pub life, getting up in the morning to get their water from the local well, serving the drunks as best she could, and staying out of the way of their hands. The palace was a different world altogether. Nothing like the bard's stories and nothing like the life of a peasant. There were rules about who could be seen where. Servants weren't to be seen in the main halls except when serving their master. Nobles weren't to be seen in the back halls, and if they were, there was a king's ransom to be made selling that information. Everyone had their place and knew what that place was. And everyone always tried to have more than they were supposed to have by manipulating and sneaking around.

Allay didn't really have a place here. She was something the rest of the palace didn't really understand. Even the servants who had decided she was worthy of being a friend didn't understand her part in the palace game. Allay couldn't help them. She learned of the game faster than any other new member of the palace only because she could listen in on people debating their next move. She knew that was cheating, but they would do the same to her given half a chance. The game was really all about cheating.

Playing the game as a servant was nothing compared to the complexity the lords insisted on. She could hear them all thinking through their options as they strolled the halls, waiting their turn for the interview. In all their calculations for how to turn this situation to their advantage, not one of them took Allay into account. Not one. She should laugh at them for that. They were smart enough to consider all the other servants and which ones were in the pay of which lords, or so they thought.

It was, Allay thought, a good thing she didn't really play the game. The temptation to cheat would be too great.

She slipped through the little door at the back of the audience chamber just in time to hear Silvanie call for the first lord. Another of her maids stood where Allay usually did, pretending to understand what she was there for. She gave Allay a look of relief when she saw her peeking out of the curtain. Silently, as only trained servants could, they

148

changed places.

I'm here. Allay assured Silvanie as soon as the other maid was gone.

Good, I wasn't sure what to do without out you, considering Callay is the second of the lords this morning.

Don't worry. I'll be here for you, Allay thought with more confidence than she had the right to feel. It was confidence she felt, though the reason behind it slipped from her mind as soon as she went looking for it.

The interview took about an hour and revealed nothing shocking. Of course the lord had secrets, but none were worthy of passing on other than the names of the servants he paid for information about the royals.

The lord was released and there was a pause before Callay would be brought in.

"Where were you?" Silvanie asked. Her voice sounded hard, but her thoughts were more concerned.

I went to the temple.

"And didn't tell anyone?"

I'm not used to being able to tell people where I'm going. It was true enough. It would also have been true to say she was too upset to think about it. Or even that it wasn't any of the princess' business when she went to pray. That last, while true, would not go over well.

"Lord Callay." The grand doors opened and the man Kayla had asked about walked in. Like all the others, he carried himself as though he were the most important person around. His thoughts were something else.

He is worried you will know about his daughters. Allay emphasized the plural.

He has just one daughter, and we all thought she was dead.

Allay looked closer. *He has two that he's aware of. Avianna who has disappeared from her tower room and he worries may have come to court with his other daughter, Marissa.* Allay tried to hide her own shock that the woman Kayla brought back claiming Cook was her mother could also be this man's daughter.

Silvanie turned her attention to the interview Sir Delare was conducting, so Allay did as well. She checked his spoken answers against the ones he only thought. Surprisingly, he didn't seem to be hiding much. He admitted to his wish that King Thorwin hadn't chosen Silvanie as the heir and that he had talked to several other lords about plans to deal with the king.

He wishes he hadn't joined Tromadin in bringing Kayla. He blames her

149

for his daughters.

Sir Delare didn't follow his worries about his daughters, but he did bring up Kayla. Though, both Sir Delare and Lord Callay referred to her only as "the green demon." Allay had to push her frustration deep to keep it out of her thoughts.

He is really worried that Sir Delare is going to ask about Avianna.

Silvanie gave a slow nod. She knew he wouldn't and was hiding something from Allay. Funny, now that she knew some people could feel her thoughts, she was getting much better at keeping them under control. Would the lords learn the same trick if they ever figured out what Allay was doing? That would make her less useful, and she would probably be sent back to the Broken Ale.

Allay wondered if she could start the rumors herself. Would she really want to go back to the Broken Ale now that she'd been part of the princess' court?

"Lord Callay." Silvanie called the man back just after Sir Delare had released him. "I'm sorry, but I have to ask, what of your daughters?"

Fear poured from the man so strong it made Allay's stomach clench.

"I don't know what you mean."

"You have two daughters, correct?" Silvanie's voice was sweet, but her thoughts were pure venom. "Avianna and Marissa, unless I'm mistaken."

Callay opened his mouth but couldn't answer.

He's more afraid of you knowing about Marissa than Avianna. Allay tried to make sense of the rest of the thoughts about Cook, who he thought of as "Lady Dressen."

"I'm sure of it now." Silvanie rose from her throne and took a few steps toward the stricken lord. "I remember playing with Avianna during the summer holidays when all the noble families came to the palace. She was such a sweet girl, around the adults, but led the rest of us into trouble as soon as we were alone."

Callay stood his ground only because he couldn't get his feet to move.

"Funny that I don't remember Marissa. She is of noble birth, though her mother worked in your kitchen." Lady Dressen and Cook were more than just different names for the same woman. There were stories about her, though of low rank among the nobles. "Whatever happened to Marissa?"

"She chose a peasant life," Callay croaked out.

"Did she now?" Silvanie raised a hand to the guards at the great doors. One of them slipped through the door. "I would have thought you'd bring her back into the house after the death of Avianna. It is ill luck to have no marriageable prospects to create alliances."

He's relieved you don't know about Avianna.

The door opened and the guards announced Ladies Avianna and Marissa of House Callay. They entered, Marissa lending her arm to her sister. Marissa was still dressed in the manner of a peasant, though the dress was clearly new. Avianna wore a dress more elaborate than Silvanie's.

"I was mistaken." Silvanie grinned at Lord Callay. "It seems both of your daughters are alive and well."

"Your Highness." Sir Delare bowed as he spoke. "I do believe this represents a treason."

Sir Delare winked back at Allay. *This was planned.*

Now Callay turned white as could be. If he wasn't so frozen, he would have fallen to the floor.

"Explain." Silvanie smiled at Sir Delare. If they had been peasants, that kind of look would be flirting. Here, it was part of the game. A sign to their opponent that there was more going on than he was currently aware of.

"A lie to the royal family that affects the line of succession," Sir Delare said. "With Avianna still alive and able to produce heirs, we will have to recalculate. Not to mention the funeral and all the expenses that were sent from the royal coffers to show proper mourning for a member of the line who had not in fact deceased."

"That is a treason." Silvanie nodded. "And what of concealing a daughter of the line by calling her a peasant and keeping her from court?"

"Another treason." Sir Delare nodded to the guards, who stepped forward. "Of course your punishment will have to wait until after the coronation, since we don't have a seated monarch at the moment."

"What of my sons?" Callay screamed as the guards took his arms. "This is not their doing."

The poison of Silvanie's thoughts dissolved into images of the two boys attempting to sneak into the palace. They were followed and taken when their intention to kill their sister became clear. "You'll have plenty of time to talk it over with them," Silvanie said. "Be sure he is placed within shouting distance of his sons."

Who will run Callay County? Allay watched them take the lord, whose thoughts had become as incoherent as his screams.

"Lady Callay, if she can be found." Silvanie sighed. "Kayla

didn't have anything to do with that, did she?"

Allay shook her head. *She only took Avianna through a portal. She left the rest of the house untouched.*

"If not, Avianna is refusing, but Marissa would be willing if a suitable match could be found." Silvanie smiled. "Smart of her. I wouldn't want to run a county on my own either."

But you have the whole country to run.

Silvanie sighed. "I don't want to do this on my own either, but I'm not going to hand it over to a lump like that, now am I?"

CHAPTER THIRTY-TWO
Lord Corawin Tromadin

Corawin wandered the halls of the palace, trying to find some lord worth talking to while avoiding the ones he didn't want to see. It was disturbing to see how many women were strolling the halls out of season. Women belonged at court only during the spring season when all nobles were to come together and make arrangements for future weddings. Then the women went back where they belonged and the men were able to get back to the business of running the country. Now, with so many women, and most of them he didn't know, he was constantly distracted and drawn into conversations that made no sense.

"You must think it odd," one woman had told him, "that there has been no mention of Marissa Callay."

Of course he thought it odd there would be mention of Marissa Callay. There was no such woman, and what did he care of romantic fantasies? More disturbing were the number of third and fourth sons who were being mentioned as possible successors should this Marissa choose them. Since when did any daughter of a lord think she had the right to choose in the first place, let alone an imaginary one?

Escaping from one such conversation, he'd run into Lord Farthingay.

"With the coronation so soon, you'd think all the council would be working toward making it a success." Farthingay always liked to start conversations somewhere in the middle. This was about as coherent as Corawin had ever found the man.

"There is still some question as to the legitimacy of the succession."

"Oh, didn't you hear?" Farthingay looked as though his father had just promised him a pony. "The gathering of priests has begun. It will only be a matter of time before Silvanie is confirmed as heir."

Corawin felt the air stick in his lungs. "When did that happen?"

"Yesterday." Farthingay grinned. "Well, the priests gathered yesterday and a note was sent to Silvanie just after dinnertime. They'll make the official announcement soon. I don't plan to miss public prayers tomorrow."

"Public prayers?"

An outburst of screaming followed by several guards running toward the audience chamber prevented any further discussion of the priests' choices for making the announcement about the succession. If they weren't going to make the announcement until tomorrow morning, he still had time to change their minds, or the situation.

For now, the commotion gave him the chance to get away from Farthingay.

"Stand back," a guard commanded, using his spear to force the people back against the wall.

More guards came to block them all into their places while a small group dragged a man past screaming incoherently. The man was dressed as a lord, though the guards were rough enough with him that the coat was half dragging on the floor and the shirt underneath ripped to show indecent amounts of skin.

They were almost past when Corawin caught sight of his face. Lord Callay, twisted in fear and hate, was a wonderful sight to see. With that loose end all tied up, he could focus more readily on the remainder of them. He would need to consolidate his power quickly, of course, and deal with that damned green demon. But she'd been conspicuously absent from all sightings and even rumors for days. Perhaps she had found her own end. That would be a pleasant surprise.

"Lord Tromadin?" A page too small to be called such bowed before him.

"Yes?"

"A letter in your name."

The boy handed over the sealed note with another bow and disappeared between the legs of the others still milling about after the scene.

The seal came from the Temple Of Odran. The temples never bothered to distinguish where the temple was located when they sent such missives. How frustrating. He would have to read it, but not where Farthingay, or anyone else, could be glancing over his shoulder.

Odd, too, he thought as he threw the latch on the door to a sitting room he found unoccupied. Why would the letter have been sent to him at the palace rather than his city residence? Priests were strange creatures at the best of times and only useful when their ability with magic made a plan easier. Even then, he wasn't so sure they were worth the aggravation.

He made a second check to be sure the room was empty before cracking the seal.

Come at once to the temple nearest the palace.

It was signed by the high priest himself.

The Temple of Odran held a special place in court, being the chosen temple of the royals for as long as anyone could remember. Never mind that Odran ruled over travels, but then who better to oversee diplomatic missions? If the high priest of Odran wanted to see him, then there was more hope that he could sway the decision over Silvanie.

Get her out of the way and he would have a clearer sight to the throne himself. He wouldn't have to kill everyone on the list above him, just enough to give fear. If all the rest stepped out of the way... Oh yes, things were progressing nicely.

* * *

The acolytes at the gate were expecting him. As it should be if the high priest had sent for him. Still Corawin was encouraged by their presence. The young lad brought him directly to the main shrine within the temple, where the old priest knelt in prayer.

Corawin chafed at having to wait, though he didn't say anything in the temple. Gods always outranked humans. Even the king bowed to the gods. Corawin could bite his tongue and wait his turn.

"Come pray with me." The old priest spoke without moving from his position before the altar.

Corawin hadn't prayed in years. Not since he realized the gods didn't talk to anyone but their priests. If that were the case, then he would leave the praying to the priests as well. Nonetheless, here he was in the temple with the high priest. He could pretend to pray if that would help his cause.

"Odran is with you," the priest said when Corawin dropped to his knees before the altar. "Though you are not with him."

"It is hard to be with a god," Corawin said.

"Yet you called on his services."

Corawin nodded. "The country was in need."

The priest nodded. "The succession troubled you. It still does."

Corawin sighed. He needed to choose his words carefully. One did not lie to the high priest of the god of travels if one did not have to. "Silvanie, though of royal blood, is not an appropriate choice for the throne. Perhaps if she had been well married, there would be cause to accept her as the blood line, knowing her husband would lead the country."

A silence fell over the temple like a blanket. Even the old priest's breathing became muted.

"A journey is not about the destination, but rather the effect it has on the traveler." The priest quoted from the standard liturgy.

"And that effect is guided by the man at the head of the procession." Corawin did remember his prayers. "A princess raised to be the wife of another ruler does not have the skill or knowledge to lead a country through the troubled waters of international politics. She will be dismissed by the other kings and ineffective at dissuading them from bringing their armies against our land to take what they want."

The priest knelt in silence. Corawin wondered what game he was playing at. Did he really seek the advice of a lord known to oppose the princess, or was he trying to persuade Corawin to change his mind?

"Then you would prefer a more militant example at the head of our state?"

That wasn't how Corawin would have put it, but it did make a certain amount of sense. Especially with the chaos of a transition brought about by assassination, a militant figure taking the throne would send the message that Greylein was not to be taken lightly.

"It would lend us strength at the end of the chaos." Corawin just managed to keep his voice even.

The priest dropped his head to the floor, ending the prayer in reverence for the god. Corawin followed his example, then helped the old man to his feet.

"Ah, I'm afraid my journey is getting ever harder." The old priest smiled his thanks to the lord. "So you think yourself the kind of presence that will keep our neighbors on their side of the border."

"Yes." Corawin nodded. "My record as a leader is clear for anyone to see."

"That it is." The priest nodded and started walking toward the back entrance to the temple. "Your record is quite clear and just a bit on the frightful side. Do you suppose that might be a problem for you should you take the throne?"

Corawin jumped for joy inside. Then they were thinking of putting his name forward as the heir. Since the temples had been invoked, it wouldn't matter what the genealogy said. The gods could and would pick whom they wanted for the throne. No one could dispute that.

"There are negatives to every plan. Of course there will be

some who find my leadership harsher than they wish. They will not impede my ability to lead."

The old priest laughed. "Such confidence."

"Confidence is the most important trait in a leader."

"Of course it is. The second most important is humility."

Corawin nodded. There was no way he could point out his own humility without being seen as a braggart.

"I heard the announcement of the heir would come tomorrow during public prayers."

"And you are well connected, I see. However, tomorrow may be a bit soon. Not all gods are as quick to respond as we would like." The priest put a hand on Corawin's shoulder. "When it comes, it will be during the public prayers. The whole country should learn at the same time who their next leader will be. That way there will be no confusion or chance that rumors will confuse the matter." He squeezed his gnarled fingers into Corawin's flesh with surprising strength. "I would suggest you take the news with your wife and sons beside you."

Corawin nodded. Yes, that would be the best. Let the others think he did not see his name would be the one on all the priests' lips. Let him be called back to the capital for his own coronation. It would prevent the vicious rumors and undercurrents long enough for him to seize power and prevent their petty squabbling from getting in his way.

"Thank you, Principe. I appreciate your time."

CHAPTER THIRTY-THREE
Kayla

Kayla stepped out of her portal onto the ledge outside Crystal's cave. It was concealed in the foggy illusion the dragon maintained to hide her presence from the humans. From inside the illusion, it appeared Kayla was nowhere. All around her was undifferentiated white; nothing visually told her she was standing on anything at all. She should have paid attention to this when she first arrived.

Keep the pink demons at a distance. They aren't like you any more than the citizens of Kralt.

Oh, that's just the homesickness talking. Crystal's bright attitude flooded her mind. *Now come in before you worry yourself to death.*

The illusion faded just enough for Kayla to find her way into the grand hall of an entryway. Kayla smiled to herself as she trekked through the vast cave to the even bigger main chamber. The fog pulled back, allowing her to see the table and fire pit in the middle of the cave. Crystal's head hovered several body lengths above the floor while the rest of her remained hidden in the fog.

Why do you hide yourself?

"Because I want you to focus on this part of me." Crystal lowered herself to the floor. "It's hard to have a good conversation when your partner is trying to contemplate your size."

Kayla laughed. "You know your head isn't exactly small either."

"Such blunt words." Crystal lowered her ears in mock shame. "You could hurt someone like that."

"Then they need to be hurt." Kayla laughed. "Or maybe I'm just not the person they need."

Crystal clicked her tongue. "You are exactly who they need. There are too many lies floating around this world as it is."

That was true too. "I don't understand," Kayla confessed. "I don't understand the games they play to decide who gets to have power. Or why so many of them just accept they weren't born to the game and let their so-called leaders heap cruelty on them."

"Well, it didn't take you long to find the hardest questions of our age." Crystal laughed. "Humans, as a species, are a special kind of crazy."

"It makes no sense."

"It does, if you think about it long enough and let your thoughts get thoroughly tangled first. But if we are going to do that, I should make you dinner."

With that, Crystal lifted herself beyond the clouds and out of sight completely. Kayla was left to her thoughts. Not a position she really wanted to be in at the moment. The confusion about the game Silvanie played and the sincerity with which Allay defended her. Allay didn't even understand the game yet was unwilling to consider it wasn't the only way to govern.

"Don't tie yourself in knots over them," Crystal warned over the screams of the rabbit.

Kayla winced at the way her dinner was being made. "You were listening to my thoughts?"

"Of course, dear, you weren't shielding them from me."

"I suppose I can't complain. I'm in your house."

"Would you complain if you knew I was listening most of the time?"

What? Kayla checked her mind. She had thought her shields were in place. She was used to keeping her private thoughts hidden deep, or she had been.

"Don't worry so much." Crystal laughed. "You are the most interesting thing I've seen in generations of humans. Of course I pay attention to you. And don't forget I am not like your Felani family. My mind is different."

That was truer than Kayla wanted to admit. She had thought too much of the dragon as a piece of her home. It was time she realized there was no piece of home here.

Crystal returned with two rabbits hanging from her teeth. Even in death, the pain of their transformation was evident in their bodies.

"It is a cruel way to die." Kayla took the rabbits from Crystal's mouth.

"No worse than starving to death and much shorter in the suffering." Crystal puffed a small fire into existence next to the stone table. "I'll let you cook them the way you like. I'm not much of a chef."

Kayla laughed as she skinned the rabbits. "No, I suppose you wouldn't be."

"If you want cooked meat, I would introduce you to Blaze. He's got the taste for roasted sheep and the power to make it a real habit." Crystal's tail brought the copper teapot over to heat by the fire. "I don't see it myself, but then I'm not that skilled with fire."

"Skilled enough." Kayla set the first rabbit to roast in the coals of the fire, then turned to slice the other one into strips for smoking.

"Starting fire on dry wood is nothing. Starting a fire without wood at all is another thing altogether." Crystal added a plate of mixed greens to the little table and a copper cup for tea. "Blaze has that kind of skill."

"So he's another kind of dragon?"

Crystal laughed. "Oh heavens, you really don't know, do you?" Dragons, Crystal explained, took their power from the sign of the moon when they hatched. Blaze was hatched under the fire moon, so his primary power was fire. While Crystal had been hatched to the ice moon. Blaze's clutch mate waited for the harvest moon to crack her shell and took the power of plant life for her own.

"Is there a blood moon?" Kayla asked. Kayla herself was found under a blood moon and was believed to have the heart of a warrior because of it.

"There is." Crystal became quiet for a time. "We don't allow hatchlings to take the power of a blood moon. They give us a bad reputation."

Kayla knew it wasn't that simple but let it go. Instead, she concentrated on getting the strips of meat arranged around the fire to dry quickly in the smoke.

"I've more meat frozen if you'd like to preserve it in a way you can maintain," Crystal suggested.

"Why frozen?"

"It keeps it from rotting, and I can't eat it once it's been transformed."

Kayla took the rabbits, sixteen of them, and began the process of cleaning them. "So many," she murmured.

Crystal tossed her head a bit. "I was trying to refine the transformation so it wouldn't kill the rabbits. A breeding colony would keep you stocked for life, and we wouldn't have to hear them scream."

A noble thought, though doomed to failure. Changing a creature's nature that far was more than even the prepared could handle.

Kayla smiled and continued her work. This stock of dried meat would keep her well fed for months. Longer than she hoped to live here, but a sweet gesture all the same. She was able to lay it all out just in time for the roast rabbit to come out of the fire.

Over dinner, Crystal told more tales of life on this world and the strange creatures who lived here. There were great serpents in the sea who were distant cousins of the dragons. No magical ability to speak of, but their skill at manipulating the water itself could be devastating to the silly humans who dared sail the seas without offering proper tribute. Great birds of the mountains in the south born of fire. This far north they were only told of in legend because they were impossible to capture. Any net or cage would simply burn around them.

By far, the strangest creature in Crystal's repertoire were the humans. Intelligent enough to wield the power and manipulate the world yet silly enough to organize themselves in harmful ways.

"It hasn't always been so," Crystal assured Kayla when she snorted about the silliness of the humans. "When I was still a hatchling, most humans were still wandering the world in tribes. They followed the leaders who were strong enough to keep the group alive. A bad leader soon lost her tribe."

"As it should be," Kayla said with more conviction than she intended.

"So that is the way of your family." Crystal spoke softly, as though trying not to break a delicate egg. "For the humans, it had its problems as well, and they moved to the cities as quickly as they could be founded. Humans thrive on their crops and domesticated animals, so they stopped moving about so much."

"And lost their minds in the process." Kayla scoffed. "Just because they don't move as tribes doesn't mean they have to stay with a leader who abuses them."

"No, it doesn't." Crystal nudged the teapot toward Kayla like a mother trying to calm a child with a distraction. "And it didn't, not right away."

Crystal spun a story of short generations and the knowledge that is lost when not used. The abuse didn't start until the people no longer remembered how to live without a house or a garden plot. When they had become so tied to the land they could barely imagine life on the move. They had learned so well how to bring the resources they needed to them there was no need to remember how to go to the resources.

There were some who remained as mobile as their ancestors, but they became dependent on the stationary humans for their food and well-being. These merchants lived from town to town. Others preyed on the stationary humans and moved to keep ahead of the law. Still, they couldn't live as their ancestors had, completely mobile.

"Such a sad story," Kayla said.

"And one you found in your own history, did you not?"

"What?"

"You complain about the people who look like you, the ones who build their cities in the trees. Do you really think they lived in place before they learned to build cities?"

Of course not. They had to have moved about in search of their resources at some time in the past. But then they founded their cities and also lost their minds.

"They didn't lose their minds." Crystal shifted to bring her great eye level with Kayla's head. "They developed a different sense of priorities."

"Those priorities are making it hard to see how they survive." Kayla paced between the table and the fire, pretending she was checking on the rabbit and returning to her dinner, but she actually did neither.

Crystal watched her through three rounds. "Does it bother you so much?"

"Of course. Doesn't it bother you? They are going to kill themselves off or make themselves weak. It's a horrible situation." She expanded her pacing around the cave as she ranted. "I can't stand to see them being so stupid when I know they are capable of so much more."

Crystal pulled the fog back farther and let Kayla storm around the cave until her rant had run its course.

"Did you know all of Callay's staff left the house rather than face his wrath when you took his daughter to court?" Crystal spoke quietly into the silence.

Kayla stopped her pacing to stare at the dragon.

"You were the spark that started the fire," Crystal said. "They were not happy, but they didn't see what to do. When you came, it was like a fire started from friction. Just one little spark will flare to something much greater."

One little spark? The goddess had talked of a change as well. She expected Kayla to bring on the change they couldn't make happen themselves. A spark, a catalyst, a change, and here she was, as different from them as could be. She would be the spark, and change would come. More than just a little nudge, Kayla would change this world until even the gods didn't recognize their people. That is the price of bringing her here.

CHAPTER THIRTY-FOUR
Lord Corawin Tromadin

Rumors swirled about Lord Callay for days, each round becoming more and more ridiculous. Corawin didn't have to *act* shocked to hear about his two daughters suddenly becoming available for marriage. He, like everyone else, had believed the funeral for Avianna, if not the death, and had never even heard of Marissa. It wasn't acting when he asked what would become of the now shamed lord.

He was relieved to hear that final judgment on matters of treason to the crown would have to wait until after the coronation. Not that it would be any better for Callay when he took the throne; it would just be more satisfying to be the one to declare the man a traitor and have him executed. That and knowing he and his sons were stuck in the dungeons like common criminals for the next two weeks would be fabulous.

Of course, he never put all his hopes in just one plan. Aside from the many stories he'd spread to explain why he should be the next king, he had scandals mapped for everyone above him in the succession. The one piece he had yet to bring under control was the green demon. She had the bad habit of popping up somewhere just long enough for people to see her. By the time his men got there, she was gone, leaving no trace they could follow. It was time to bring the problem back to those who had caused it.

"Principe Haverey," the doorman announced as he ushered the priest into Corawin's office.

As with all priests, he entered the room as though he were the one to have summoned Corawin. That air of importance they gave themselves grated at Corawin more than the silliness of their rituals or even the thought that all magic belonged to the temples.

"You wanted to see me?" Principe Haverey didn't even attempt to bow.

Before looking up, Corawin finished the calculation he was working on in the books for his private guard. "We have a problem."

"We?" Haverey had the decency to look a bit nervous. Or maybe he'd noticed Brace in the shadowed corner of the office.

"We. You and I, together, have a problem." Corawin replaced the quill in its stand with exaggerated care. "Me because it came from my county and therefore I must clean it up, but you because you were the one who promised the spell would bring me the champion I needed. Instead, it brought a demon who has done everything except what I needed it to do."

"You told us the requirements, and that is what you got. Anything after that…"

Brace shifted in his corner. Corawin loved the way he was able to instill fear just by adjusting his weight.

"Well, since you know the demon that well, it will be no trouble for you to trace it now." Corawin leaned back in his chair.

Haverey swallowed hard. It would be difficult, no doubt. The creature they'd summoned was nothing like the requirements Corawin had given them. It was capable of doing things no other mage in all the kingdoms could do. Rumor had it that not even the strongest of priests were able to see the methods she used to control the blue holes that appeared around her. Some even said she didn't control them; she simply used them when they came. Corawin didn't care how it happened. All he knew was those blue holes only appeared around her and they were making it impossible to track her.

"It's not so simple as you make it sound." Haverey reached his hand to the god token he wore under his robes.

"I really don't care. You will help my men trace that demon or I will report you to the temple."

"That spell was at your request."

"Oh, I meant I would report you for using those poor girls." Corawin smiled his most predatory smile. "I have to protect my people, after all. Their mothers are so upset and their fathers… How will they ever find reasonable matches after you?"

"But I didn't…" Understanding dawned slowly on his face. The priest knew it would be nothing for Corawin to find abused girls who would testify tearfully that it was the priest who caused their condition. "I'll do what I can."

"You'll do better than that if you want to die in one piece." Corawin waved the priest away.

Corawin waited until the door was shut to let out his breath. This little distraction was becoming more of a headache with each passing day. Why didn't the demon just use one of those blue holes to return to hell and be done with it?

"Captain Traggel wishes to speak with you, my lord." The doorman bowed low for his interruption.

"This had better be good." Corawin glanced at Brace, who showed nothing. "Show him in."

The captain bowed and stayed down. "I have a disturbing report."

Corawin sighed. "What kind of report?"

"A squad just returned from the tax collection duty. Three small villages are empty, sir."

Well, that made no sense. "What do you mean empty?"

"There's no one and nothing there. I mean, the houses and barns and things are there, but the people, harvested crops, animals, they're all gone."

"They were attacked?" Of course there would be bandit raids. The country was in chaos.

"No, sir, there was no sign of fighting of any sort." The captain described how the towns had been found as orderly as if the people had really just packed up and left. They had taken the time to be sure everything was ready before they simply departed.

"The soldiers couldn't find a trace to tell them which direction they'd left either." The captain bowed even lower, quivering in fear.

"Of all the blazes…" Corawin slapped the table. Just like all the scenes Brace had described when they followed a rumor to the green demon. Gone without haste and no trace of direction. "It's that damned demon."

"Sir?" The captain stood without permission, but Corawin didn't care.

"What does it want with peasants?" Corawin turned directly to Brace. "What does it want?"

"Who's to say?" Brace shrugged. "Demons are irrational creatures. Perhaps she needs their souls."

That was the most ridiculous notion Brace had ever given him.

"You've been tracking it, don't you know more than that?"

Brace closed his eyes briefly before stepping forward. "I've heard just about every rumor there is to hear about that demon of yours. The peasants call her an angel sent by the gods. They claim Kethry created her. Lords and merchants claim her a demon possessed by Thibben to cause chaos. She has been seen among the griffins as often as with people. Some even say she has the ear of Princess Silvanie. I've heard rumors too that she's given herself to the dragons to be their messenger among the people. If I didn't know better, I would think you had me chasing an entire race of demons around this country."

For once, he bowed, low as was proper his station. Then he left without leave, keeping his reputation intact.

Corawin growled after him that it was the last time that man would be given leave to behave so inappropriately.

"Gather your guard," Corawin yelled at the captian, "and find those people. They belong to the land, and all they have is mine."

CHAPTER THIRTY-FIVE
Allay

The interviews with the lords were over. That should have been the end of it, but no one confessed in voice or thought to having hired the assassin. Allay was sure some of the lords were capable of hiding thoughts and they should be looked at again. Lord Tromadin, for example. His mind was filled with all kinds of plots, most of them aimed at keeping Silvanie from the throne. Yet he claimed not to have hired the assassin, even thought it. Why would he hire an assassin when he'd put his money and effort on calling a champion? There were other thoughts in his mind that Allay couldn't understand. And some she didn't want to think about ever again.

Allay shuddered just thinking about what she'd seen in the minds of the lords. It made it hard to look at the servants happily chatting over breakfast.

"What're you gonna do now?" one of the maids asked, handing Allay a fresh sausage-filled biscuit. "They're done talking to the lords."

Princess Silvanie still needs me. She almost added the part about listening for thoughts, but that part was supposed to be secret.

"Of course she does." Another girl giggled. Allay caught the image of her kissing Silvanie before she clamped her mind shut.

"That's enough." The grand woman of the kitchen smacked the giggling girl with a ladle. "You don't talk about the princess that way."

Allay ducked her head and hid the biscuit in her skirts. She wasn't hungry anymore. The sex-filled thoughts of the maids were more than she could handle. It was almost worse than in the minds of the working men who came looking for relaxation at the Broken Ale.

169

In their minds, it was to be expected, but these girls were supposed to be innocent.

They weren't innocent. Every last one of them sold information to one lord or another. A few even sold to foreign visitors. Not one person in the whole palace lived only on the wages afforded a royal servant. Those who didn't have information sold anything else they could. Those two maids were known for sleeping with one lord and selling that information to another. They were so open about it they shared tips for avoiding pregnancy. So they all thought Allay would be part of it as well, just as soon as she learned the game.

Allay gave herself another shake as she passed from the kitchens into the servants' halls. She didn't want to play the game they played. She didn't think of it like a game the way they did. It was too easy to imagine what would happen if all the people of the city conducted their business as a game. The city would fall apart. Just getting water up from the well would be more expensive than most of the shop kids could afford.

"What's got you all somber this morning?" Princess Silvanie asked.

Allay didn't remember walking into the audience chamber. She still held her sausage biscuit in the folds of her skirt. She was supposed to have eaten it before the morning session started.

The other servants. Allay let Silvanie see the memory of that morning's breakfast.

The princess laughed. "I can see where that is a bit disturbing, but it isn't anything unusual."

Other than I wouldn't do that. Allay shook herself again. *It's all the bribing and dealing and get what you can with what you've got. It's…"* She pushed her imaginings of what the city would be like for Silvanie.

"Isn't that what they do?"

Allay let her mouth fall open. Silvanie's innocent question revealed more about the problems of the palace than those of the country. *No, it's not. Shopkeepers set their prices and that's what people pay. There's some room for negotiation of course, but not like that.* Allay shared a day at the Broken Ale with the princess, emphasizing how real everything she remembered was whenever Silvanie tried to reject it. *It's like they tell us in the temple. Be honorable, be true, help those who need the help, and you will be helped when you need it.*

Silvanie shook herself this time. "It's hard to believe how different life can be."

It's not so hard if you think about the differences themselves. Allay had thought about those differences since the day she first met Kayla. A

170

creature who could speak with her mind and thought it only natural to have friends like the griffins. Her life had been so different, and she struggled to understand the people here. Allay couldn't help her because she knew the lords were different than the peasants, but not how. Now she was the one who came to a new world where the rules were nothing like what she was used to. *Maybe you should spend more time among those who do not live in the palace.*

"Now that would be scandal." Silvanie laughed. Then she sighed. "We must get on with the day's business."

Allay bowed herself into her place just behind the throne. The business of the day was all the reports and visits that had been put on hold for tracking the assassin. These came from officials who were as likely as the servants to be getting paid by other lords for information.

Do not trust the tax assayer. Allay heard him think about how much he was skimming from the merchants of the city.

There is more to the problem of the farms report. The man claimed there were problems with several of the harvests. He left the problems vague but worried over them in a way that should have been clearer.

"What kind of problems?" Silvanie pressed him.

"The harvests just aren't as big as expected."

"Why?" She leaned forward.

Allay saw the empty villages in the man's head but let Silvanie tease it out of him. He struggled to keep the full extent of the problem hidden, sure if the lords were given just a little more time, they would have their peasants back and the harvests would be found.

"They're just gone." He wailed at last, dropping to his knees before the princess. "No one knows where they go, but in almost every village, you can find signs that the people are packing. They are carefully gathering all their things and the crops. None know where or how they will leave, but they are ready should the time come."

Ask about stories. Allay wanted to see what he would think of.

There were stories and then stories. Most of them he didn't believe. The peasants talked of a dragon that flew over the village. That was the sign it was time to leave. The angel would come and tell them how.

They're talking about Kayla.

Silvanie turned in her chair to stare at Allay. *How do you know?*

Crystal told her she could make a choice that would change the course of history. The old dragon asked her to think carefully about it.

When was that? Silvanie's thoughts were all jumbled with memories of a priest telling her as a child that things would change in her lifetime.

171

When Kayla first appeared. Allay thought of the day she met Kayla. What a change that made in her life.

"Thank you, that is all." Silvanie walked out of the chamber before the minister of farms could get to his feet. *Come.*

Allay knew this would get interesting.

CHAPTER THIRTY-SIX
Kayla

The children met Kayla about a third of the way from the forest to the village. They ran up and circled her like the street children back home. These kids were as hungry for the stories and treats Kayla brought as the ones back home. Kayla didn't have any treats, but she had plenty of stories.

"Are you a witch?"

"Are you an angel?"

"How did you get here?"

Kayla smiled, careful to keep her teeth hidden. These children were excited but could easily become frightened if she wasn't careful. "Didn't you see the dragon?"

The dancing stopped while they all looked at her with wide eyes and open mouths.

"You came with the dragon?" one small boy asked.

"I did."

"See, told ya." The little boy stuck his tongue out at an older boy.

"That's just a story," the older boy retorted automatically.

The rest of the children laughed.

"It is a story." Kayla started walking toward the village. "And it's true."

"Then the winter village is true?" A small girl whose dress was covered with mud tugged at her trousers.

"Yes, the winter village is true as well."

You still call it a village. Blaze laughed in her head. *There are enough people in my cave to make it a city.*

Do you regret helping me?

He laughed with the thought of children on his back. His favorite part of the whole operation.

"Nana says you can make all the lords disappear," the mud-covered girl said.

"Don't say such things," an older girl warned. "They'll hear you."

"Doesn't matter."

"I can't make them do anything," Kayla said. "I just want to get their attention."

"Why would you want that?" One of the older girls shuddered.

Kayla didn't want to imagine why she would have that reaction. She just added it to the list of reasons she hated the lords. "So I can tell them they are wrong."

The children laughed again. They danced around her all the way to the village, then disappeared. The adults of the village didn't come to greet her the way all the others had. If she hadn't seen them running about when she flew over on Blaze, she would think the town had been abandoned already.

Can you see what's different here? Kayla sent to Blaze while she continued to walk through the town as though she didn't notice anything was wrong.

There are men with weapons among the people. Blaze's image was fuzzy so she didn't have a clear picture to compare to what she was seeing. *Take care. There is menace and admiration for you among these people.*

Blaze wasn't as skilled as Crystal at reading the minds of humans, but it was better than not having a dragon there to help out. *Keep me informed if anything changes.*

You mean like a pair of boys who just found my hiding place?

Keep them safe.

Kayla found the people of the village gathered in the town square, huddling together in small groups around the edges. Also around the edges were men in dark armor, holding small blades with excess caution. Poisoned. In the center was a man she almost recognized. His armor labeled him a guard of Tromadin, like the others, but there was something just a bit different about the way he carried himself. More of a hunter than a guard.

"You do know poison won't hurt me." Kayla spoke to the man in the middle.

"It'll hurt them." He shrugged.

An old woman tried to step forward but was held back by other

174

villagers.

"You're the one who's been tracking me?" She took her answer from the slight flicker of surprise in his eyes. "Well, you've finally found me. What is it your master wants you to do with me?"

He paused to glance at the dirt before catching her eyes again. "Kill you."

"That should be fun." Kayla had yet to test her skills against the fighters here. She'd seen their practice and the way they moved in their armor. Kayla preferred the loose-fitting trousers and shirt she'd adopted from the peasants. The freedom of movement gave her more flexibility to avoid getting hit. She thought that better than trusting armor to take the hit. Armor had gaps and weighed you down.

He grinned at her, his hand reaching for the blade.

"Bray, don't you even think about it or I'll smack you like I did when you were a boy." The old woman broke free of her friends, tottering toward the man on shaky legs and a stick. Her other hand was raised in a threatening gesture.

"Nana, stay out of it." The man waved her back.

"I'll not have you become the most hated man in all the kingdoms." She stuck her finger in his face, almost up his nose. "I tried to raise you better than that, and look what you've done with yourself."

He raised his hand to hit the old woman, but Kayla was faster. Her portal dropped him where she could block the hit. "Respect your elders." Kayla copied all the women she'd heard warn their children since she started gathering the villagers.

He reached again for his blade but stopped when he felt her claws at his throat.

"I don't want to fight you." Kayla released him.

"Then what do you want?"

She grinned. "I want to go home."

"So you are stealing all the peasants?" He snorted at her.

The villagers grumbled at that statement.

"I'm not stealing them." Kayla shifted to a longer distance between them, like a wolf sizing up an interloper. "They come or not as they chose."

He laughed. "Peasants don't leave their villages."

"We do when there's somewhere better to go."

Kayla didn't see who shouted.

She did see the soldier moving toward a cluster of villagers who all looked guilty. Kayla opened another portal under him that dropped him next to Bray.

"The next portal will open farther away and less safely." Kayla

175

swept the square with her eyes. "It is up to the people here what they choose to do."

You are being very free with your portals, Blaze warned.

More than you know. I won't be able to open a portal to the Winter Village long enough to get these people and all they bring there.

I can't carry it all either.

I'll think of something.

The people were milling about with a little more confidence.

"Did you come to lead us to the Winter Village or not?" Nana toddled closer to Kayla now. "Or are you just like all the other stories of hope that have wandered through before?"

"I came to tell you of the Winter Village," Kayla answered. "Since you already know about it, that isn't necessary."

"The Winter Village?" Bray asked.

Kayla shrugged.

"You ninny." Nana smacked his arm. "Where do you think everyone was going?" She turned to Kayla. "We've heard your stories and are ready to go."

Kayla smiled. Other villages needed time to get ready. How many more were just waiting for her to come now that the story was out? What could she say to the woman? She wasn't going to lead them in a way that would leave marks for men like Bray to track, and she couldn't just open the portal.

Kayla! Sharl's mind touched hers with irritation. *What has you so tied up that you can't hear your friends calling?*

Of course it would be a game for the griffins.

Who among you can hear me now? Kayla thought as broadly as she could.

We can, came several griffin minds all at once.

A young couple stepped forward.

"Wonderful. Griffins will be coming shortly." Kayla spared a moment to tell the griffins the same thing, giving them the images of the two who could hear. "You two will be able to hear them. You'll need plenty of rope for any of your large animals or carts."

Bring as many of your kin as you can find, Kayla told Sharl. She sent a similar thought to Blaze.

"That's it? That's what you are going to do for us?" Nana had her finger in Kayla's face.

"You wouldn't want me to just give you direction where they can hear, would you?" Kayla pointed to Bray specifically.

"He's a good boy." Nana looked at him. "Or he was, once."

"He will be again." Kayla promised. "When all of this is over."

She looked about to argue, but Sharl landed behind Kayla with more than enough wing flapping.

You need to come to the palace. Sharl tossed her head. *What's this game?*

Kayla relayed the plan to Sharl, who fluffed her feathers in delight. It wasn't long before most of the flight had landed in the city. Competition sprang up over who could carry what. The griffins didn't hesitate to push the soldiers out of the way as they gathered everything that was needed. The young couple took to their role naturally, giving orders to gather everything.

The soldiers were soon corralled in the square. Almost everything that had been packed was gone by the time Blaze descended onto the roof of the inn, the only building in town sturdy enough for him to perch on. The two boys he'd been watching over were whooping in delight between the ridge plates on his back. Three more dragons, all smaller than Blaze, landed around the village.

For a moment, the humans were all frozen with fear. The children were the first to recover with curiosity. Slowly the adults began to move as well. The griffins had cleared the village of everything that could be packed by the time the soldiers regained their courage. By then, the rest of the peasants were seated between ridge plates and the dragons ready to fly.

Kayla stood beside Bray with the soldiers to watch them rise above the clouds. The griffins delighted in taking off in all directions until they were out of sight. Just as she turned to ask Bray what he wanted to do now, an arrow point poked her in the back. Without hesitation, she dropped the archer through another portal to about a mile above the village. The rest of the soldiers backed away except Bray.

"Don't make your nana a liar," Kayla warned. "She called you a good boy, Bray."

"Brace." He glared at her.

She nodded. "Brace." She held out a hand in their gesture of greeting. "My name is Kayla."

He took her hand without hesitation but held it tighter than she expected. "What are you doing here?"

She rejected the urge to pull away. "Tell your master I want to go home." She matched his stare with the same intensity. "If he doesn't send me there, I will take apart the system in which he has power."

"There is no way." Brace shook his head just a little. There was a hesitation that told her he hoped he was wrong.

"What happens now? This village is empty and you'll not get your taxes from the people." She gripped his hand as hard as he gripped hers. "How many more before there isn't enough to feed the soldiers. How many before he can't pay his taxes?"

"No, he won't send you home."

"Then he'll lose everything."

They stared into each other's eyes like the predators they were until Kayla was sure she could see his spirit staring back at her.

He released her hand with a shake of the head. "We'll find this Winter Village."

"And the dragons who set it up." Kayla smiled at him. "They have taken a mother's view of those peasants. You'll get yourself roasted if you try to hurt them. Your nana said you were a good boy, Brace. Prove it."

Kayla opened another portal to the palace. She gave Brace one more smile before she stepped through.

CHAPTER THIRTY-SEVEN
Allay

Allay sighed as she stepped from the bath, amazed at her new-found desire to be clean. To be honest, she'd always wanted to be clean, but living in the palace had changed her idea of what it meant. She had a fresh uniform dress waiting for her as she dried off. She also had the joy of being alone in the servant's bath. Silvanie sent her away, saying she needed to be alone with her thoughts.

Allay couldn't blame her. She'd been shocked first by the clothes Allay insisted on, which weren't really all that peasant-like since they were clean and made of comfortable cloth. Then Allay insisted on the dirt. No one would miss the princess with her pure skin. All of that was before Allay handed her the market basket and they headed out into the city. Silvanie made a lousy peasant even with Allay's coaching. People knew they weren't peasants, even if they hadn't seen her guards, who made even worse thugs than Silvanie's peasant.

All that considered, the outing was a success. No one bowed and they mostly went on about their business, snickering behind the princess' back. Allay took her to the lower town well, where the shop kids helped each other pull up the bucket. They bought the vegetables the head cook had asked for from the East City market. The "thugs" got to practice their art while Silvanie did her best not to insult the shopkeepers about the quality of their produce. They took a midday meal at the Broken Ale, where Missy stepped in to relieve the guards who were as shocked as the princess. Then they walked past tannery row. Even Allay had to hold her breath since there was only a slight breeze to disperse the smells. They wended their way through forge alley to the shop favored by the head gardener to retrieve some of his tools that were sent for repair.

"This is normal?" Silvanie asked as she struggled to lift the basket with the tools in it.

Allay redistributed the tools and vegetables between their baskets. *This is just a morning. Most peasant women would have been done with their shopping by now and to their work.*

Silvanie sighed. They still had three more errands Allay had arranged for them. She assured Silvanie that the worst was behind them, when a gang of street children ran past followed by young thugs intent on retrieving whatever the kids had stolen. They made it to the florist for that evening's displays for the royal table, a potter to commission a new vase, and finally the upper town market for the specialty herbs that weren't permitted to be sold in the lower town market.

They returned through the servant's gate after guard change, where Silvanie was treated to the leering looks of the guards who weren't aware enough to recognize her. As soon as they were in the palace, Silvanie handed her basket to Allay and ordered a bath be ready by the time she arrived in her quarters. Allay didn't need to hear the words to know she was to be absent until the following morning.

Allay spent longer than she should have in the servant's bath once all the purchases were delivered. In early afternoon, there was no one to notice she was scrubbing just as hard as the princess to remove the dirt she'd deliberately put on that morning. It was still early for the evening meal when she finished dressing. She decided to ask in the kitchen for some small duties to keep her occupied.

"What do you think you are doing?" Sir Delare caught her arm and dragged her into a small sitting room.

Anger swirled around him so intense he couldn't keep it all contained. The fierce thoughts were blaming Allay for something she couldn't quite grasp.

"What were you thinking?" He threw her into one of the puffy lounge chairs. "Taking the princess out among the rabble. They could have killed her."

They didn't. It was all she could think. His anger held her attention while fear crept out from the back of her mind.

Fear was the difference between survival and all the worse things that could happen in the streets or skies. She'd learned early to keep her fear under control. She did just that, but the fear kept building.

"You still don't understand, you silly girl." Delare leaned over her, forcing her farther into the chair. "You are nothing here. You don't understand the delicate balance that keeps…"

Allay closed her eyes, curled into a ball with her arms crossed to protect herself from his attack. She quit hearing him to focus on getting herself under control. But these weren't her fears. Something as trivial as a man of Delare's size wasn't something she worried about. She could slip from his grasp easily enough. The fear still battered at her thoughts, keeping her body paralyzed in that chair while he yelled about how she didn't matter.

Fears were large men too drunk to keep their feet under them near the fire. Her fears were of falling from higher than the palace towers, seeing a memory or plan she couldn't do anything about. Allay huddled in her mind, gathering all the thoughts that really scared her. She wove them into a shield around her mind, keeping the fear Delare pushed at her beyond reach. In the calm, she watched carefully how he was pushing the emotion-filled thoughts at her.

Allay gathered her shield into a dense wall of her own fear and pushed back the same way. His assault gave way before her force. She pushed harder, past the wall he kept around his thoughts and deeper to the place where he kept his own fears.

Something crashed, followed by silence. Allay dared to open her eyes just a bit. Delare was slumped against the wall. A chair and two tables were tipped over and a vase lay in pieces beside him, the flowers scattered over him.

The main door to the room flew open, admitting several guards. The first two became glassy eyed as soon as they saw Delare. The third looked away and came to get Allay.

"Are you all right?" He avoided looking in her eyes.

She nodded, not willing to extend her mind anymore.

"Let's get you out of here." He lifted her off the chair. He knew what Delare was and how to keep his thoughts contained. Another surprise Allay didn't have the energy to worry about now.

As he carried her past the other guards, she caught a hint of what they were dealing with. Delare's shield had been broken and all his plans and manipulations were flying about. How he found Silvanie easier to manipulate than Thorwin. He'd spooked the horse that killed the prince and pushed the king to make a public announcement. How angry he was that the assassin hadn't waited for the announcement before killing the king and queen. Allay closed her mind to it all, burying herself in the guard's comforting grip.

CHAPTER THIRTY-EIGHT
Lord Corawin Tromadin

Corawin hated traveling by carriage. If he didn't need to be seen bringing his wife and sons to the coronation, he would have let them travel on their own. The hours spent staring at his wife across the carriage from him grated more than he dared let her see. Especially not when she would be gossiping with all the other wives who would undoubtedly tell their lords an altered version that would result in a scandal he had no way of heading off.

"Shall I plan for a reception?" Giselle asked as they approached the house. She'd been blissfully quiet most of the trip.

"I would think there will be more than enough planned already." Corawin pulled back the curtain to see how close they were.

Giselle nodded. "I just want to be sure we don't damage our reputation." She kept her eyes lowered and voice quiet.

He heard the disapproval in her comment all the same. "If there is an evening we haven't been invited to a proper reception, perhaps we could host one."

"Thank you."

Her lips tipped up in a slight smile. It would be an expense unless he could arrange to be out every night until the coronation itself. She would be happy to have enough excuses to show off all the dresses she'd packed for this trip. He didn't worry about where they came from. Her household budget was done properly.

Brace was waiting for him when they stopped. Corawin ignored him until the public viewing of him with his family was finished. "Did you find her?"

They were still in the receiving hall, but Giselle and the boys took themselves away.

"I did."

"And?"

"She's harder to kill than you might think."

There was something different about the man's manner. He didn't even pretend to bow.

Corawin turned on him.

"You dare to tell me you've failed to kill the demon without even trying to show me the respect I'm due?"

Brace smiled. "What respect are you due?"

"I am your lord. You will show proper respect. Bow when you approach me. Call me sir. All those things I have let slide for too long."

Brace nodded as Corawin spoke.

"You may be a lord, but you are not my lord." He stepped forward to close the distance between them. "I've been chasing this mess you called on yourself, and one thing I've learned is that demon is a better person than you are."

"How dare you—"

"She sends you a message." Brace backed away a few steps. "She wants to go home and all you have to do is think for a moment she has finished her task and she'll be out of your life. If not, she promises to take everything that makes you think you have power and break the whole system."

"No." Corawin unclenched his fists. "She hasn't done what I called her for. If she were that powerful, she could take herself home."

Brace shook his head. "I've seen children treat her like a favored bard. I've heard people call her angel. She can command dragons and make people unafraid of them. If she says she can destroy the country, I'm going to believe her." He turned toward the main door.

"You were supposed to kill her."

"She's more skilled than I am."

"Where are you going now?"

The hunter didn't respond.

"I said where are you going now?" Corawin rushed forward to grab Brace's arm. He found himself pressed against the wall with the hunter's arm pressed against his throat.

"I'm going to find the Winter Village. And if they'll have me, I'll join them there."

Corawin fell to the floor, gasping for breath, when Brace released him. He couldn't even call for his house guard while he watched the hunter walk out the front door. He wasn't even sure what had just happened.

"Sir?" The butler was by his side, offering him a hand up.

Corawin slapped it away before pushing himself up.

"The invitations, sir, I've organized them by date." The butler bowed with the silver tray of cards held before him.

Someone here understood his place.

Corawin took the invitations and flipped through them. At a glance, it looked like they would be too busy to host a reception of their own. All the better. He wasn't in the mood to host the other lords in his home. He needed to get ready for his coronation.

"Thank you."

"Sir, a personal message as well."

"What is it?"

"A council meeting has been set for tomorrow morning at second bells." The butler bowed himself out, tucking the silver tray under his arm.

* * *

Corawin arrived early but found the council room already filled. Everyone chatted in their small groups while servants roved among them with refreshments. Council meetings were too much like receptions, Corawin thought. That would change under his reign.

"Ah, Tromadin, I'm so happy to see you've made it." Farthingay caught him on his way to the head of the table. "I was worried the plague of peasants might have you tied to your lands."

"I'm not so plagued I can't come for the coronation." What kind of king would miss his own coronation? But that wasn't announced yet. "And how are your lands?"

Farthingay set his jaw and moved off to talk to someone else. So the demon was spreading her anger over more than just his land. The peasants couldn't live on their own for long. They'd be back as soon as they remembered the protections a lord could give them. More brief conversations confirmed the demon was attacking indiscriminately among all the lands. As he'd thought, she couldn't target him directly. She was just one demon.

"Her Royal Majesty, Princess Silvanie," the herald announced, calling them all to attention.

She still wore black for her parents, as was proper. Now if she would just give up the idea that she could hold the throne and let them get on with choosing the real king for the coronation.

"Thank you all for gathering on such short notice." She spoke even before taking her place at the table. The new serving girl still followed her everywhere. "I'll make this quick, as we all have duties to get to, I'm sure."

Now she waited for them all to find their places at the table. The serving girl's eyes roved over the lords as they arranged themselves. Corawin didn't trust that girl. She would be out in the street as soon as he took the throne.

"As you may have heard," Silvanie started before they were all in place, "Sir Delare has been taken into custody for treason to the throne. I've remanded him to the Temple of Yeheri until he is capable of standing trial."

Corawin held his expression flat in the face of that news. He couldn't be seen smiling at the misfortune of another member of the court. This development could only be for the good.

"We are still trying to understand all that came to light with his arrest." Silvanie continued when the shocked noises subsided. "We'll keep the council informed of any other arrests that result from this part of the investigation."

"What about the parts he was involved with?" Lord Farthingay asked.

"There is no need to worry about the testimony you gave. It has been recorded and the records will be reviewed rather than inter-viewing all of you again." She gave Farthingay a sad smile.

"And what of the peasants?"

Corawin didn't see who asked said that.

Silvanie took a moment before answering. "The crown is aware that all counties have been affected by the peasant revolt. At this time, we have no solution to propose. Again, as we learn more, you will be the first to hear."

Corawin couldn't hide his smile. The demon was creating a crisis that would bring the princess to her knees. Not fast enough, but maybe she would learn she just didn't have the skills to lead a nation. Corawin wasn't going to be the one to point it out, though. Let her feel the stress of a king's job for just a moment and she would be crushed by it.

The room went silent. Corawin looked up to see one of the blue holes standing on the table. Most of the lords pushed themselves away from it, but Silvanie smiled. Corawin scowled. How could that demon come here like this now? He reached for his sword.

The demon stepped onto the table, wearing a peasant man's trousers and shirt belted around her waist with a length of rope.

"You called for me?" Kayla spoke to the princess.

Corawin took the opportunity of her distraction to lunge at her. She dodged him without even thinking about it and stepped on his

186

blade.

"You really thought you were better than your hunter?" She looked down at him. "Did he give you my message?"

"You haven't done what I called you for."

She kicked the blade out of his hand, sending it spinning across the table, where the serving girl caught it.

"What did you want?" The demon had her attention back on the princess.

Silvanie lowered her eyes from the demon. "To apologize and ask for your help."

The demon walked to the end of the table and jumped down to stand in front of the princess. "You're willing to do this here with them watching? Isn't that against the game?"

Silvanie nodded. "They need to see this."

The demon looked over them all. "Do they know why I've been taking their peasants to the Winter Village?"

Most of the lords were shaking their heads. Some of them were staring pointedly at Corawin.

"That one"—she pointed directly at him—"called me for a job he never got the chance to tell me about. What I found is a broken system that I just can't stand by and watch."

The demon began moving among the lords.

"Some of you simply neglect the needs of the people who are supposed to look to you for leadership." She poked Lord Farthingay in the chest. "Some of you do try and still fail to care for them." She poked Lord Barinton. "All of you have forgotten that women are human too."

She jumped up on the table to walk straight at Corawin. "And some of you have been blatantly abusing the people you should be caring for."

She didn't poke him in the chest, but rather crouched down to talk to him directly as though speaking to a miscreant child.

"For that, you have emptied our villages?" Farthingay's voice wavered between anger and fear.

"That's the point." She stood but still spoke directly at Corawin. "They aren't your villages." She turned to face Silvanie. "The villages belong to the people who live in them. The crops belong to the people who plant, tend, and harvest them. Animals are to be cared for as living beings—that is with respect—until they must give their lives. Anything a person produces belongs to that person. Anything less and I'll continue to be the demon you take me for."

"How does this system work? There is still a need for leaders, for people to run the country and make decisions." Silvanie spoke with a practiced ease, as though she had planned this from the start.

"Then you will have to provide a service to the people with the resources you want. If you want to collect taxes, you will have to provide a service for those taxes." The demon now looked around to all of the lords. "You will have to prove to all the people that you are working for their best interests."

"If we do that, will you return the peasants?"

The demon shook her head. "I'm not keeping the peasants." She turned again to Corawin. "I bring them to the Winter Village only when they ask me to. It is up to them to decide if it is worth returning to their homes or if they would rather stay away."

"Why are you focusing on me?" He cringed at the whine he heard in his own voice.

Her words were about all the lords, even Silvanie, but her eyes were on him.

"Because you have the power to send me home. Get me out of the way." She dropped to crouch in front of him again, though this time it looked more predatory than patronizing. "All you have to do is think I've done what you called me for."

How dare she call him out like that in front of all the lords?

"Send her home." Farthingay had regained control of his voice.

There were murmurings of ascent all the way around the table.

He couldn't send her home. She had failed. He wouldn't think otherwise.

Corawin leaned in to look her in the eyes. "If you are that powerful, get yourself home."

Corawin ignored all protocol and left the council. If she hated the system they had now, she would detest the one he put in place when he took the throne by force.

CHAPTER THIRTY-NINE
Allay

Allay watched the dance between Silvanie and Kayla with great amusement. Some of the lords were impressed. Most thought it had been staged right up to the moment Lord Tromadin stormed out in a fit. None of them could believe that Silvanie would have allowed that. Wouldn't they be surprised to know their princess almost cheered when he left? It only took a suggestion from Kayla that the council meeting was finished for them all to leave under the watchful eyes of the demon.

"You've gotten better at playing this game." Silvanie laughed when the chamber was empty.

Kayla dropped off the table several feet away from the princess. "It's not a game." She pushed a chair out of the way.

There was a seriousness in Kayla's thoughts deeper than her manner suggested. Allay stepped back. She would need to do something to calm their nerves. A drink would help, and there were goblets still set on the side table.

"Politics is always a game." Silvanie matched Kayla's mood. "It's the stakes we tend to forget."

"I hate politics," Kayla declared

"So do I."

Allay watched them laugh lightly. Their moods were still very intense, but the tension eased a little. They were both spilling thoughts of all the things they hated most about their experiences with politics. Kayla's were hard to understand, filled with green people in strange clothes that probably meant something. Silvanie's were mostly thoughts of lords who thought only of their own power.

Allay grabbed the goblets she'd filled and hurried back to the table. She handed the water to Kayla and a mild wine to Silvanie.

"I thought you wanted to be queen." *Thank you, it's cold.*

Allay smiled at the way Kayla was able to split her attention like that. *It's from the ice bath for the wine.*

Silvanie took hers with a slight nod. "I don't want to be queen."

Kayla snorted. Her thoughts turned toward the way Silvanie fought to return to the palace and how she played the game with the lords.

Silvanie wasn't like Kayla thought. Allay had seen how Silvanie chafed against the need for so many plots and subtle dealings. She hated that she had to listen to every word to find all the meanings in a lord's response. Even with Allay's help, she feared she would miss the one clue that would keep her from getting trapped in one of their plots.

"It's true." Silvanie held the goblet in front of her. "I don't want to be queen, but I cannot trust any of them to be king. So I will do what is needed for my country." She lifted the goblet.

Kayla's ears twitched as she watched the princess.

It's an oath. You have to touch her goblet with yours to acknowledge it. She wants you as her witness.

Witness? For an oath? Kayla raised her goblet as well. They clinked the cups lightly.

Now you take a sip, Allay directed, being sure to fill the thought with all the obligations that went into accepting the oath.

All of that just so she will keep her promise? Kayla accepted the custom, though she didn't understand it. *And if she doesn't do it, what then?*

Allay shrugged. Who would think of breaking an oath witnessed and accepted? *That is up to you.*

Kayla sipped. "Now that you've promised to take care of your land, how do you plan to do that?" There was skepticism in her voice. Her thoughts were of the people in the villages. There were stories Kayla shied away from, but the faces of the people stood clear in her mind.

"I'm hoping you will help." Silvanie set her goblet on the table. "I don't know my own people as well as you seem to."

Kayla laughed. "What makes you think I know them?"

Silvanie's thoughts mirrored Kayla's, though the stories were clear and the faces lost in shadow. They were stories Allay had known from before.

Allay faded back, listening to both their words and thoughts. Silvanie trying to convince Kayla to help, while Kayla doubted she could be of service.

Allay didn't have to see Kayla's thoughts of her Jarron or the gang of children she considered hers to know what she was really worried about. She didn't think about them when she countered Silvanie's assumptions. She thought of how little she understood of the people here. She thought of the large cats she called family and how much different this world was from that one. Her words said nothing of her home.

"I cannot help you." Kayla spoke with a low tone of anger. Her claws flashed in and out of her hands. "My goals are not yours."

She must try to get back to her lover. Allay broke in. *She has to at least try to get home.*

"What?" Silvanie turned suddenly to stare at Allay.

Allay stood straight and looked back at the princess. It took everything Allay had to keep her eyes from dropping to the floor.

She has a life that doesn't belong to this country, or this world. Allay pushed the words and faces carefully into her mistress's mind. *None of us can ask her to give up that life, to become dead to her family, just to make our lives easier. Not you, not the gods, none of us.*

Allay felt the presence of other minds in the room. So the gods were listening. Let them hear.

Kayla didn't choose to come. Allay continued, broadening her focus to be sure the heavens understood as much as the princess. *She fought the magic that brought her. She refused the task Lord Tromadin wanted of her. For that she has become stuck. We cannot forget she is more foreign than any visitor.*

You've gained skills as well. Kayla's mind calmed into a feeling of love and admiration. *I have to wonder what story you are hiding now that you've gained control.*

Allay pulled back, closing off thoughts of Sir Delare. She pushed those memories deeper into the parts of her mind she didn't look at if she didn't have to.

"You want help with understanding your people?" Kayla took Silvanie's attention back. "You have your adviser." Kayla swung her arm toward Allay, sending the princess' attention straight back.

Allay held herself up, not looking directly into Silvanie's eyes this time, but not dropping them to the floor either.

"I need someone who can think of more than what is and what has been," Silvanie said. "I can't create something new for my people with only the old traditions to look at."

Kayla grabbed her goblet off the table and held it in front of her the way Silvanie had. There was a shift in her attitude Allay couldn't put words to. It was like a decision made long ago had come forward to

191

reassert itself in Kayla's mind. "I do not wish to stay here longer than I must, but as long as I am here, I will give you what I can to make this a better country." She lifted the goblet.

Silvanie stood shocked for a moment, then took her goblet and touched it to Kayla's. They sipped, sealing the oath.

There is a name for someone who has made that oath. Allay let her thoughts be heard by both. *Queen's own.*

CHAPTER FORTY
Kayla

Kayla could have opened a portal to anywhere else in this world and been gone rather than standing on this stool while women poked and prodded at the fabrics around her. Allay hadn't warned her that becoming the queen's own would involve uniforms and rituals. She had to be properly dressed for the coronation, but not in a uniform. The clerks were very clear on the point that a queen's own couldn't be appointed without a queen. The ladies of the sewing circle thrilled at the opportunity to dress "the princess demon."

The dress was something that would never be worn again if Kayla had anything to say about it. In fact, it might never be found again. They were being far more reasonable in the creation of her uniform.

Tradition says the king's own is to be clothed in a uniform that is both alike and different to the royal guard. Allay slipped into the sewing room. *There are no women in the royal guard so no need for dresses.*

I thought I was supposed to be something other than tradition, she grumbled. *Women in the royal guard shouldn't wear dresses anyway. It would hinder their movements.* Kayla thought of a woman trying to defend herself in a full ball gown.

Allay laughed, still unnoticed by the women with needles huddled around Kayla. *Are you ready for the ceremony?*

"I will be when they finish with the details."

The women turned with flushed cheeks to see whom she was talking to. Their faces turned even redder when they saw the queen's adviser in the room. They weren't sure whether to rise and bow or just bow from their knees, creating a scene that amused Kayla until she saw the darkening of Allay's cheeks as well.

"You should stop bowing and finish your task." Kayla would have preferred them all to be equals, but these women weren't ready for that yet.

Silvanie must give you a gift, a token of your promise, at the ceremony. Allay came to stand directly in front of Kayla but far enough back to be out of the way. *Traditionally, it would be a specially commissioned sword.*

Kayla shuddered. She'd seen what a sword meant in this land. Unlike those carried by the Krinna, a sign of the protection for the clan, here a sword showed the violence of the hierarchical system. Lords carried fancy swords to claim their rank and intimidate the people. Their soldiers carried practical swords designed for the violence they were hired to perpetuate.

"No, I couldn't accept a sword."

Nor a dagger or any other weapon. Allay nodded along.

"What else could she give me?"

Allay shrugged. *That's as much as tradition can tell us.*

"What about a necklace?" the lead sewing lady suggested. "You could use some decoration since you won't let us sew it on the uniform."

"A bracelet wouldn't get in your way either," another suggested.

"I don't want to be decorated." Such things were signs of intimacy that she just couldn't feel here.

What would you like? Allay tilted her head to look at the uniform from a different angle. *It's a bit loose, isn't it?*

"If your soldiers want to fight in restrictive armor, let them." Kayla rolled her shoulders back, feeling the freedom the sleeves gave her.

"You may step down." The women all moved back and stood. A couple of them stretched discretely.

Kayla shook her head. She would tell them to care for themselves, but they would just ignore her and turn red. She had to remember they wouldn't change just because she told them to. Even the peasants in the Winter Villages didn't really change their understanding of the world.

You know they don't think it's finished. Allay imagined the uniform with more decoration than the ladies had suggested.

"We've talked about that." Kayla led Allay out of the sewing room. "They may want all that nonsense, but it wouldn't make sense for me."

Allay smiled. Her own dress had become rather more decorated than it had been. She was still getting used to being dressed almost as brilliantly as a noble woman. *You can get used to it.*

I don't want to get used to it. Kayla would have been even happier to keep her loose britches and shirt with just a belt to hold it all together. She hadn't really gotten used to the way Kraltans dressed, and that seemed light by comparison to what Silvanie and the rest of the nobles wore daily.

There is an army in the forest. Sharl's mind interrupted her thoughts. She sent images of men in dark armor filling the spaces between the trees.

What does that mean? Allay had a look of panic on her face, but no emotion leaked into her thoughts. She was getting quite skilled in controlling them.

It means Lord Tromadin didn't take his loss well. Kayla had been waiting for his next move. She hadn't expected this or that he would be able to field such a large army.

What should we do? Allay let a little of her worry through this time.

Go tell Silvanie what is coming.

Tromadin wasn't acting alone, but he was leading this. Neither the royal guard nor the city forces were ready for this kind of assault.

What are you going to do?

Come up with a surprise of my own. She didn't want to call on the griffins again, but they wouldn't be expected.

Allay nodded and ran as fast as her skirts would let her. Kayla turned more slowly toward the room high in the east tower to gather her thoughts.

The peasants would have fun fighting the lords. Sharl imagined them giggling as they dropped rocks from the backs of griffins.

I'm not sure fun quite fits, but it would be surprising. Surprise was about the only thing they could count on. They didn't have enough trained soldiers to wage a standard war, which of course Lord Tromadin knew too.

Griffins aren't the only ones full of surprise. Sharl thought of the wolf packs that roamed the woods.

That was an interesting thought. Bring all the citizens of Greylein to the battle and show the lords what they were really dealing with. *Take as many griffins as you can to the Winter Village and bring the peasants close. Be ready by first light, but stay out of sight. Surprise doesn't work if they know you are coming. And anyone else you can think of too.*

Sharl sent a thought of pure delight. It was a new game to her and her kin. The peasants would be something else.

CHAPTER FORTY-ONE
Lord Corawin Tromadin

"Sir." The soldier's voice cut through Corawin's dreams. "The moon has set and the first light is on the horizon."

Corawin woke quickly. "Good, be sure the rest of the camp wakes as well."

"Yes, sir."

Corawin pulled himself out of the bedroll, feeling all the lumps and bumps of sleeping on the ground. He wouldn't be so uncivilized if it weren't worth the surprise. No other commander could have brought so many soldiers so close to the capital so quickly. That little girl they dared to call queen wouldn't have time to even review what guards she had left, let alone develop a defensive plan for the city. Not that she would have any clue how to do that. This coup would be over before noon.

"Report," he called as he stepped out of his tent. The one luxury he'd brought on this venture.

A squire began fitting his armor while soldiers all through the camp scrambled about their preparations.

"All is quiet, sir." One of his captains snapped to attention. This man was fully armored already, probably part of the night watch. "All we saw were the normal patrols on the city walls. There was music and lights from the palace until just about an hour ago. We suspect they were celebrating an appointment of some sort."

"You don't know which appointment?"

"Nothing our spies told us about." The captain bowed. "Though we did miss one report."

Corawin stood so the squire could fasten his chest plate, though he wanted to slap the captain for such negligence. "Which report was missed?"

"A page in the palace was supposed to send word last night, but nothing came. He hasn't been a reliable source, so we haven't been planning on his information without corroboration."

A page? Corawin winced that they had to stoop that low to get a spy in the palace.

"Very well. We'll attack just before dawn as planned. Begin moving soldiers into position."

"Sir." The captain began barking orders to the men, some of whom were still only half dressed.

He had to remind himself that this plan didn't depend on a well-trained army, only overwhelming force. It would have been better with the kind of discipline he was used to in his guard, but that wasn't going to happen with so many raw recruits and mercenaries of un-determined skill. As long as they could point their swords in the right direction and follow orders, they would do. The skilled units he held in reserve for the final push. Silvanie would keep her best guards around her, and he didn't want to do too much damage to the palace if it could be helped. After all, he was planning to live there.

The gentle glow of the predawn light made it easier for men to find their gear and get to the edge of the forest. Corawin approached the line where they would be seen with caution. Men were already crawling through the grass toward the city walls. They were making the grass move in unnatural ways, but the idiots of the city guard hadn't seen it yet. Get enough men out there and it wouldn't matter. There'd be too many too close for the city guard to fend off and the royal guard would have to split between the palace itself and the rest of the city.

"Sir." A young soldier approached with a bow. "Some of the men are concerned about the flight of griffins who live in this field."

"What's to be worried about?"

"Won't they attack if we get too close to their nests?"

Stupid concerns. "Stay away from the nests. They aren't hard to find."

The soldier bowed and left. Corawin had to remember these were not his best soldiers. They were men who could be thrown at the opposition without worry. If they died, he didn't have to pay them. Corawin watched the advance of the soldiers as far around the city as he could see. The order to begin must have reached the far side by now as well. Yet another way to spread Silvanie's forces beyond their capac-

198

ity to defend the city.

He laughed when he thought of how upset she was going to be that her little soldiers weren't able to keep things as neat and tidy as a maid kept a room. She would probably cry over the death of some peasants who got in the way too. Silly girl.

"Sir, they are opening the gates." The captain handed him a spyglass.

That they were. The great iron grates rose slowly into the wall above. There were even peasants waiting patiently for them to open.

"They suspect nothing," Corawin muttered.

"As planned." The captain smiled.

"Ready for phase two," Corawin ordered.

The smile disappeared and orders were shouted to the men. Corawin kept his eye on the guards at the gate, but they didn't take any notice of the noise or the men crawling through the field.

Something felt wrong about that. He looked closer at the guards at the gate. Their uniforms hung from them as though they weren't properly fitted. They held the spears stiffly, not with the practiced ease of a man who had trained with such a simple weapon. Looking farther, there were no sentries above the gate or archers ranged on the wall. This wasn't just incompetence.

Too late, the call went out for the attack to begin and the men in the field jumped up to rush the wall. Those still waiting in the forest ran forward too. The attack was on, but no one was fighting back. Now even the guards at the gate were absent.

"Your horse, sir." His squire handed him the reins. The stallion tossed his head, making the armor jangle.

Still feeling there was a trap about to spring, Corawin mounted his horse. His elite soldiers came to his side. They were ready for whatever the girl had to throw at them. Even a trap wouldn't stop them from gaining the palace.

"Remember the goal. Leave everything to the others. We ride for the palace," Corawin shouted.

"All hail King Tromadin," the men chanted in return.

He spurred his horse forward, and all hell broke loose.

CHAPTER FORTY-TWO
Allay

Kayla's idea of a battle plan was like nothing the bards' tales had prepared her for. First the servants who were too old, young, sick, or weak to fight were given leave to party until nearly dawn. In fact, they were specifically told to keep the palace bright and loud enough to be heard in the forest. Messengers were sent around the city to warn the people of the impending battle. All capable fighters, though, were pulled to the palace and anyone who wished it was offered sanctuary within the palace walls. Those who wished to fight were told to be sneaky about it.

"Don't do anything a normal soldier would do." That was the command Kayla had sent with the messengers.

Silvanie, Allay, and those lords still at the palace were ordered to an early bed. The soldiers of the royal and city guards were also ordered to keep the guard in the night to a minimum so most would be well rested by morning. The palace kitchens were employed to have a simple breakfast for all ready before first light.

It has started. Kayla's view of the fields around the city woke Allay. There were so many soldiers crawling through the tall grass that Allay didn't know how they were going to fight them off.

Wake Silvanie and be sure she dresses to ride. Kayla sent an image of the queen in white on the back of Crystal.

You are kidding.

She's on her way.

Silvanie was already awake when Allay opened her door. She didn't argue about the choice of clothes Allay pulled from the wardrobe or the simple porridge her other maid brought from the kitchen.

"Are you sure?" she asked when Allay urged her to hurry.

You don't want to miss all the fun. Allay couldn't help but think like the griffins. If it were just a game, it couldn't be scary and she wouldn't have to hide that fear from everyone around her.

They made it to the balcony overlooking the grand courtyard just as the first shouts came from the fields. Men's voices rose in a primal yell all from outside the walls. The courtyard below was filled with men and women who all looked toward the walls then back to their queen.

Give them something to cheer for. Allay pushed Silvanie forward.

"They think they are winning." Silvanie spoke in a deep and booming voice. "They think that because we've let them take the easy stuff. We let them take the wall. They spent time working out a plan to get into the city, thinking that was the hard part."

The people laughed.

"They weren't counting on us. On all of us, those of you standing below and those who chose to stay in the city. They are going to find out what happens when the people, when you, say no. When you look at a leader and decide he's not worthy. They are going to find out what it really means to fight."

The crowd erupted into cheers.

"We will fight."

More cheers.

"And they…" She pointed over the wall. "They won't see it until it's too late."

Allay felt her ears ring with the power of the cheers.

Is she ready? Kayla prodded Allay.

She's talking to the people.

Kayla drew Allay's attention to a cloud moving across the sky. *Her steed is ready.*

By "steed" Kayla meant Crystal, who still maintained her camouflage out in the sky. Crystal insisted on coming out. Kayla insisted she remain hidden until the time was right.

It's time. Allay included all of Kayla's instructions for where to stand and what to expect.

"Is this really necessary?" Silvanie's thoughts were filled with fear and excitement.

Kayla says it'll be the safest and strongest place for you. Allay embellished Kayla's plan.

Silvanie stepped back from the edge of the balcony and managed to remain regal while she dropped through the small portal Kayla opened beneath her feet. Then she was gone, so was the portal, and Allay had to assume Silvanie had arrived safely on Crystal's back.

Look up. Tell them to look up.

Allay braced herself for the effort of pushing her thoughts into that many minds. Then realized it would just be easier to point. Some looked. Then they nudged their neighbors and soon everyone was looking to the sky where a great white cloud vanished leaving a small white dragon in its place. The dragon grew quickly as it descended toward the castle until it covered most of the sky. It swept close enough for people to see Silvanie standing between the horns on the dragon's head.

The sounds from around the city changed. In the courtyard, the people, guards, and servants and peasants all together cheered. From the city, there were screams of terror mixed with the hoots of ruffians and cheers of others all coming together.

"Griffins," someone yelled.

There were griffins all over the sky, far more than had ever played in the fields around the city. They wove and dove in dizzying displays of aerial skill. It was more than just skill; they were carrying people. Allay wished she could be out there with them.

You haven't practiced, Sharl said. *Dropping rocks in the right places isn't as easy as it looks.*

You've been practicing?

Not so loud. It's a surprise. Sharl left off with a laugh.

"They're coming," a guard at the palace gate yelled. "They're on horseback."

Clear the gate, Allay ordered directly to the men around the gate. *Let the horses in and seal it behind them. Clear the courtyard.*

Allay stayed on the balcony only long enough to confirm that Lord Tromadin rode with his men.

He's here, Allay sent to Kayla. *I'll get him to the audience chamber.*

Keep yourself safe, Kayla responded.

She was out there, somewhere, guiding the battle in ways no human could expect. She'd promised a surprise for Silvanie, and already she'd brought out several. From the peasants willing to fight to the griffins. Even getting Crystal to carry Silvanie through the battle.

A great roar made her turn back for a moment at the door. Six more dragons of varying colors appeared over the castle and swooped down on the city. That would be another surprise.

Allay found Tromadin and his men in the great hall, amid several bodies. The smell of blood made her gag. The sight of one of the black-armored men shoving a soldier off his sword with his foot made her want to scream. Instead, she hid behind a column to catch her breath. There were eight of them with the lord. She would have to split them up somehow.

A quick peek around the column only made her look at the bodies again. Not all of them were soldiers. She looked away before she noticed which of the maids had been so unlucky.

"Where is that girl hiding?" Lord Tromadin's voice reverberated off the marble of the hall, seeming to come from everywhere.

Allay smiled to herself. Kayla wasn't the only one who could surprise them. She imagined hearing someone running down the hall away from them and pushed that thought into all of their minds.

The queen isn't here. She tightened her focus to just the lord.

"Who said that?"

"What, sire?"

Allay hit them again, this time with a memory of children playing in the streets.

"Children?" one of the men asked.

"It's a trick."

Another round of the children running through the halls had them looking in all directions.

Over here. Allay stepped out for just a moment to catch the lord's attention.

"There." Tromadin pointed his sword at her. "It's her little pet."

Allay ran as fast as her feet would let her in the billowing skirts of her uniform. She understood Kayla's objection now. She skidded around corners, keeping just ahead of the men in their armor. She had to stop at the doors to the audience chamber since they were closed. These great doors were meant to be opened by men, not children.

The lord wasn't the fastest of the group. A man with dark eyes under his helm bore down on her with his sword leading the way.

SLEEP. She pushed the order as deep into his mind as she could reach.

He fell in a tangle of arms and legs, rolling toward her with alarming speed. Allay pulled the door just wide enough to slip through.

It wasn't enough. A hand grabbed her arm and pulled her back. Her body slammed against the door, opening it farther.

"That's enough out of you." Lord Tromadin glared down at her.

"Leave her be."

Kayla stood in the center of the chamber.

CHAPTER FORTY-THREE
Kayla

Kayla had to force herself to keep loose and ready to move. Her stomach wanted to turn inside out at the sight of Allay in the hands of that man. Rather than let her go, Tromadin pulled Allay closer so he could put his sword to her throat.

Keep still, Kayla warned Allay. "She's not the one you want."

"Where is the girl, Silvanie?" Tromadin asked.

"Out where a good leader should be. Leading her people against yours." Kayla moved toward him, keeping her body upright but otherwise letting her predator nature show itself. "You should know by now, you've lost."

He laughed.

Kayla stalked forward another step.

"Keep coming and I'll kill this girl."

Kayla smiled. "So you are smart enough to fear me." She stood just a bit straighter, with her hands open, and stepped back a bit. "I wonder how your men feel about that?"

Six men stood in a semicircle around the lord, half in and half out of the room. Their stances suggested they weren't so sure about this situation.

"They are loyal."

"Really, you are afraid of an unarmed woman while threatening a child?" Kayla shook her head slightly. "I'm still new to this world, but I'm pretty sure those are not the qualities good soldiers look for in a leader."

He pushed Allay from him. "They look for the one who can

offer them the most power."

They aren't so sure about him because of the children, Allay thought as she ran for the far end of the room.

Children?

Allay made her hear children running and laughing in the hall outside. A good trick.

"So if I suggested I could make them immortal if they just brought me enough children to sacrifice, they'd be mine to command?"

The soldiers shifted just slightly away from the Lord.

"Or maybe I could tell them I can summon more demons, since that helped you get power."

Tromadin stiffened just a touch.

"You do know how to make me go away." Kayla started walking forward again. She had enough power left to open about three portals just long enough for someone to fall through. She wished she could do enough to remove the other soldiers. They weren't standing close enough together for that.

"I won't confirm you've done what I asked for."

"It's just a thought." Kayla continued to advance on him. "One little thought and I'll be gone. Haven't I caused enough trouble? It's not like you are afraid of lying."

He just stood his ground and glared. The others though had lost their fighting stances.

The soldiers expect to be paid for this from the royal coffers when he takes the throne. Allay added a feeling that they weren't so sure of his victory now.

"I've taken your peasants so they aren't available for you to abuse. They aren't there to pay your taxes. How are you going to pay for their services?" She gestured to the men behind him.

One of the soldiers stepped back.

"I'll pay them from the royal coffers," Tromadin said.

"Didn't you understand? You've lost this battle." Kayla grinned. "This is still Silvanie's palace. Those coffers are hers, and I'm pretty sure she isn't going to lend you coins enough to pay them." Kayla's smile widened. "You see, those peasants I took are right now dropping rocks on your soldiers from the backs of griffins. That is unless the dragons have convinced your army to surrender already."

The soldiers shifted away from the lord.

"You know…" Kayla shifted her gaze from Tromadin to his men. "It's likely all the rest of the army have given into the dragon fear and are being taken into custody."

Tromadin is beyond angry. Kayla didn't need Allay to know she was

206

getting to him.

Kayla was almost within striking distance of Tromadin's sword.

"You know your problem?" She turned back to Tromadin. He was shaking ever so slightly. Not the quiver born of fear, but that brought on by anger. "You think only human men are worthy of respect. You forget that human women have the same minds you do. Griffins are intelligent too, and dragons aren't brute beasts."

He lunged as soon as she was within distance. Kayla blocked the blade and came in close. He wasn't where she expected him to be when she swiped with her claws. She jumped back out of the reach of his sword. This would be more of a fight than she thought.

"Your problem is you don't respect the ways of this kingdom." He advanced on her with a menacing stance, his sword now steady between them.

She dropped into a hunting stance. In the steppe, it would have brought her lower than the grass. Here it made her weird. Weird was really all she had. Keep him guessing. Frustrate him with moves he can't anticipate. Maybe she could irritate him into sending her home.

He attacked again, but she sprang over his thrust. She wasn't fast enough on the way down and missed kicking the sword out of his hand. She turned the landing into an attack of her own, striking at the fasteners of his armor. She couldn't hurt him with all that metal in the way. There were ways to kill him around the armor, just as there were ways to kill a deer without having to chase it for a day.

Killing him wasn't her goal.

He pressed his advantage as soon as she landed. He wanted her dead.

They danced around the room, trading blows and jabs. He kept up with her easily despite the heavy armor. Or perhaps it was her own weakness showing. This world was as much a burden on her as that armor on him, maybe more so.

"You could just send me home." She caught her claws between the plates of his armor and ducked his wild swipe at her.

"Never." His voice was breathy.

She reached for the power to open a portal, but there was none. She had used it just to keep her own strength up. No way to put this battle aside for another day. The point of his sword grazed her shoulder. She needed to put an end to this before long.

"She's weak. Attack now," Tromadin ordered his men.

Kayla couldn't face them all. Not without the power. Only two of the men came forward, but it was enough to distract her. She took her eyes off Tromadin for only a moment, but he used that against her.

The tip of his sword sliced into her thigh. She didn't feel the pain so much as miss the ability to use that leg. She just managed to dodge his next thrust, but her strike back had no effect.

If she couldn't slow him down, he'd succeed in killing her. That would solve his problem as easily as sending her home. Solve his problem, not hers. She shifted and dodged his attacks without the chance to counter. She wasn't going to be able to block him much longer.

"Give it up," he growled as she launched another attack.

Kayla let him slide his sword into her shoulder so she could bind his blade. The pain of the sword was easy enough to ignore; the pain of losing to this man, this pink demon, brought a scream from her throat as she sliced through his.

She fell back, no longer able to ignore the pain nor summon enough strength, or will, to push his dead weight off of her.

"Congratulations." A man, not quite human, reached a hand down to her.

He wore a simple outfit of browns with sturdy boots and a cloak thrown back over his shoulder. His skin could have been the pink of humans but was dusted brown to match his clothes. His eyes glowed golden as he looked at her with a somber expression.

She took his hand and felt him lift her mind out of her body. "Odran?"

"As smart as Kethry told me." He smiled.

"You are the god of journeys." She stood before him but could look back on herself dying under the weight of that idiot.

"You aren't dying." Odran circled around. "He is, which is why I can be here."

"Then why talk to me?"

He laughed. "Because you are on a journey as well."

"Am I going home?"

"Eventually."

"Not very powerful, then, are you?" She turned away.

The audience chamber appeared to be frozen in time. All but one of Tromadin's men were sprawled on the floor, the last staring wide-eyed at Allay. That girl didn't know how to worry about herself, did she?

"Not as powerful as the humans believe," the god admitted. "Not powerful enough to bring you here on my own. That took all of us."

"So you can't send me home on your own either." She stepped toward Allay, wanting to protect her. "How many gods do I need to convince?"

"As I said, all of us. Twenty-three the world over."

Kayla snorted. "And you aren't going to tell me what I need to do to convince them, are you?"

"I can't, because we don't know."

She turned to glare at him. "So the humans think you know more than you do too?" Kayla wondered that a god would be so honest with her about the tricks he played to keep his power over the humans.

"They make assumptions. We only know what happens in our temples or is seen by our priests." He came to stand before her, just a little shorter than she, with his hands held humbly in front of him. "You are different."

"So you won't let me die and you won't send me home." Kayla stood before the god, his head bowed as though setting her above him in rank. The temptation to accept that rank flittered across her mind and was gone.

The god let out a snort of laughter. "He coated his blade in distilled hedgelock. I have nothing to do with that."

"In that case, I have an oath to keep."

She imagined herself back into her body. The pain wasn't as strong as it had been, and she had strength enough to slide out from under him. She could feel the tingle of the hedgelock in her thigh and shoulder.

Are you hurt? Allay ran toward her.

"Stay back," Kayla warned.

CHAPTER FORTY-FOUR
Allay

Allay found Queen Silvanie holding court in the grand ballroom the morning after her coronation. It was just past first bells, but the room was filled with people hoping to spend a moment with their new queen. Allay thought it was better to hold these sessions so soon after the battle in the ballroom. It was bigger than the audience chamber. Besides, Kayla wouldn't let anyone in there until she finished cleaning it. She had set the locks so no one but her could enter.

"Good morning." Silvanie greeted her.

The people all around Allay dropped their heads, assuming she was some sort of high born.

Good morning, she responded. She practiced moving her lips just a bit when she projected. It kept her from scaring the people.

Her new uniform, or rather manner of dress, looked a bit too much like the dresses of the ladies of the court. The clothes went with the new title Silvanie had given her, "queen's adviser," to be sure everyone knew what kind of person she was. It didn't work really. The lords still thought she was just a peasant doing a job while everyone else assumed it meant she'd become a noble. Allay tried to follow Kayla's example of not caring what anyone thought of her, but it was harder than it looked.

"It is a good morning." Silvanie inclined her head to Allay when she stepped up to the dais. "What's the mood this morning?"

I'm tired, but they are mostly still wanting to thank you for being queen. Many have stories of how they helped in the battle they wish to share with you. Several have losses they want you to recognize.

Silvanie sighed. "Let's take a mix. I can't handle the losses all at once. A loss, then a story. Leave the thank yous to the end."

Allay nodded.

"Any word on when we'll get the audience chamber back?" Silvanie asked before Allay reach her mind out to the crowd.

Nothing yet.

Kayla's mind wasn't blocked. It was just very focused. She wasn't thinking about when it would be done, just what her next step would be. More specifically she was avoiding thoughts of how she was stuck here. With the death of Tromadin, his spell was no longer wrapped around her. It had dissipated without being completed. She threw herself into cleaning all the poisons from the stains in the audience chamber to distract herself.

Though she did spend some time with the seamstresses yesterday.

"That is a good sign." Silvanie smiled. "Did you get the canteen?"

I have it. Allay let Silvanie see what Dan and Allan had been able to create from the images Crystal pulled from Kayla's mind.

"That's Jarron?" Silvanie asked. "He suits her. What are the words?"

There is always a way. Crystal said it was a common phrase among Kayla's people, though the letters were those of the small, dark-skinned people she called "Krinna."

"Maybe we should just…"

Allay looked up when Silvanie's voice trailed off. There Kayla stood at the back of the room in the formal version of the uniform of the queen's own.

"I'm ready." Kayla's voice sounded hollow over the silence that fell over the crowd. She gave the feeling of having made a no-win decision. "I'll take your oath."

Silvanie grinned across the crowd as though they weren't there. "Let's hear it then, your oath."

"I swear," Kayla stepped forward and the people bowed themselves out of her way. "Oh stop it. Don't you bow for me."

The peasants who were gathered stood without hesitation. It was the lords and other dignitaries who glanced at Silvanie for confirmation. Silvanie didn't give them anything.

They will have to learn on their own. Silvanie warned before Allay could fill in the gap.

Allay stood as still as the queen and waited for Kayla as though there were no others in the room.

Only when everyone was standing and there was a path all the way to the dais, Kayla stepped forward again.

"I swear that I will do everything in my power to help your people, all your people, live well in this country." *Whether you like it or not.*

Silvanie nodded to accept the oath.

"I swear I will do everything in my power to find a way home for you."

The queen wasn't supposed to offer an oath in return. That was what the canteen was for. Allay kept her thoughts to herself. These two powerful women had just pledged to change the world, what more was there to say?

Kayla stepped up to the dais to face Silvanie directly. Neither one could bow to the other, but they could and did lock eyes for long enough to make even Allay fidgety.

"There is always a way." Silvanie spoke so only Kayla and Allay could hear. She held out the canteen for Kayla to see.

The only outward sign of the emotional turmoil that picture stirred inside the green demon was a single tear that ran down her cheek. Kayla's hands were steady as she took the canteen, but she held it with great care.

Thank you.

www.ingramcontent.com/pod-product-compliance
Lightning Source LLC
Chambersburg PA
CBHW072050170626
46813CB00004B/1289